AUTUMN
NIGHT
Whiskey

WILLOW WINTERS

One man loved me when I didn't even like myself. The town whispered that we were star-crossed lovers … among other things. He was my first love, but so out of reach with where fate had taken me.

With a little girl to look after and a past I wished I didn't have, things were never going to be easy when it came to my life in this small town. Let alone my love life.

At least that's what I thought until he showed up. A former flame who still ignited a part of me I thought had long gone.

As if life wasn't complicated enough.

Two men want me, two men kissed me … and my heart is split between them both.

Autumn Night Whiskey is book 2 of a contemporary romance duet. *Tequila Rose* must be read first.

AUTUMN NIGHT

Whiskey

Magnolia

Three years ago

TWO ADVILS SIT IN THE PALM OF MY HAND, and I'm quick to throw them back and wash them down with a bit of tea. It's the perfect temperature. A black and white caricature of a Boston terrier wearing pink glasses with a fifties-style bow adorning her ear looks back at me from the ceramic mug as I set it down on the counter. Quietly. Everything is done oh so quietly so I don't wake up Bridget ... again. Please, Lord, let my little girl sleep for more than twenty minutes. Unless she's on top of me, her little fists holding on to my shirt, sleep is hit or miss.

Everyone keeps telling me to let her cry it out, but

if she's crying, so am I. I can't stand the sound of her wailing. It's like she's begging me to just pick her up and hold her. Ugh. I don't know that I can do anything right, but I can at least hold my baby girl.

I'm grateful for a moment to myself, though. Just a moment.

I shouldn't even have caffeine this late, but I needed something soothing. Something that would calm me down after the day I've had. Or maybe I should say, the day *we've* had.

The sudden *knock, knock, knock* at the front door has me sucking in a breath and holding it in as I race to answer it on the balls of my bare feet.

Just as I'm peeking through the peephole, Robert raises his hand.

Don't you dare. I seethe with apprehension and rip the door open as quickly as I can before his knuckles rap on the door again.

"Shhh," I scold him, finally letting out that breath. "She's asleep," I say, stressing the word *asleep* although he has no idea how much it means that my two-month-old is sound asleep in her rocker and letting me have a single moment without her screaming at me.

Every cry carries with it the idea that I'm a bad mother. That I don't know what I'm doing. It all reinforces how much I miss my mom. I have never missed her more in my life. She would know what to do. She'd be right here to help me if she could.

The breeze from outside is chilly, forcing me to wrap my arms around myself. The satin pajama shorts and camisole sleep set I've got on barely covers me. The thought reminds me it's probably stained with milk and I've been wearing it for at least two days straight.

"Sorry." Robert's hushed answer comes complete with that puppy dog look in his eyes he's had off and on for the better part of a year since I've been home. A gust of wind tinged with salt from the sea licks by us as I stare back at his pale blue eyes, wondering why he's here so late. Crickets chirp behind him as he scratches the back of his neck and whispers, "I just stopped by because I heard you were looking for me."

Opening the door wider, a gesture that he can come in, I leave him there while I gather up rent. He didn't make me pay a deposit, and he didn't come for last month's rent either. Ever since I moved in here, after selling the last of my father's estate like the court ordered, I've known that I owe Robert more than I can repay him. Not just moneywise, either. His help with navigating the legalities of what my father's scandal left me with. His help with the funeral even … I can't repay all of it, but I can at least give him rent.

The chirps and nightlife chatter are silenced as he steps inside and closes the door. My back's to him, but

I hear it all as I stare down at the cash in the kitchen drawer.

His frame is far too large for that doorway. He's always been taller than me, but lately he's felt … distant. Everyone has. It's then I take him in.

He's the same as he's always been, devilishly handsome, yet charming. Tall but not overbearing. It's his strong shoulders and even stronger jawline that give him such a masculine appearance. Combine that with a clean and crisp cologne, simple khakis and a navy collared shirt, he's the sight of a Southern gentleman if there ever was one. Complete with baby blue eyes and dirty blond hair that used to make me weak in the knees. It all still does.

The creak of the floor as he makes his way to me, causes me to wince and turn my back to him so I can stare at the baby monitor.

Back to the present. Back to now and rent being due.

With no movement on the monitor, I count the money again. It's all in twenties, but the full six hundred is there. I know a two bedroom in this area goes for more than that, but it's what Robert told me rent would be. Next to it is a pile of paid bills, each marked off with a permanent marker after I mailed in the checks. Adulthood is expensive and I never knew every little thing could add up so quick.

"How are you?" Robert asks after taking in a deep sigh. Shoving down the anxiety over my finances, I turn back to him, getting a good glimpse at the guy I used to love. He was my best friend for so long. I dreamed for years of what our future together would be like.

White picket fence and blue shutters. A border collie puppy would be our "baby" for the first few years.

Never would I have guessed I'd be renting from him while taking care of a little girl on my own.

"I have the rent," I finally say, although it doesn't really answer his question. I pick up the stack of twenties and add, "I'm going to start working soon, so there's no reason I can't pay." It hurts. I can't deny that to see him and remember what could have been physically pains me. I love my baby girl, though, and that keeps me standing upright with all the pride I can manage.

Biting down on my lower lip, I hand over the money. I loved him with everything I had once. That changed, obviously. When I came back home and he tried to be right there beside me like he hadn't shattered my heart, I told him to stay away from me. And when I found out I was pregnant, during all the madness and all the anger I had with what my father had done … I told him the baby wasn't his. I shouldn't have explicitly said it, even though I'm almost certain there's no way Bridget could be his. We used protection every

5

time. The one-night stand I had after Robert dumped me … I'm almost certain we didn't.

I'm more than aware I don't deserve any kindness from Robert at all. I've pushed him away time and time again, but still, he comes back.

"You don't need to—"

"I really appreciate you letting me stay here, but—"

"If you're going to cut me off, I'm going to cut you off," he bites back with a tension I'm not used to and strides into the kitchen, eating up the distance between us. He's too close to me, smelling like the memories I wish I could escape back into and staring at me with a gaze I know all too well. Too self-assured in being right here with me, when I haven't asked a thing from him.

"Please," I whisper and try to keep the tears from coming. I don't even know why I'm crying at this point. I'm exhausted, an emotional wreck, and there's plenty that's dragged me down with celerity. Right now, all I want is for him to hold me and tell me it's all going to be better, and that's the last thing I need. Empty promises with no logical reasoning. "Just let me pay you."

There's very little money left over from my father's estate, and that's being held up in the lawsuit filed by my father's girlfriend, who's closer to my age than his. I don't know what he ever saw in her. There's enough in my bank account to last another two months and, in the meantime, I'm selling everything I can. Renee's going to help me with my résumé and I'll get a job. My degree will wait, even if the tuition bills won't. I've got a plan and my life right now isn't what I thought it would be, but I'll make it work for me and my baby girl.

Holding out the cash with my arm fully extended, I keep him at a distance.

"I don't want your money, Mags," Robert answers simply, slipping his hands into his pockets, refusing to accept it.

"There's no reason for you to let me stay here for free." How can I look at him, a man who's got it all, a man I feel like I betrayed, a man I lied to, and not feel inferior? It's all I've felt for nearly a year, but I hate him for making me feel this way all over again, simply by standing in front of me, not taking the money I owe him.

"You lie," he tells me, and my entire body goes hot.

"I'm not a liar."

"You said there's no way she's mine," he says and his voice is tight.

With my lips pressed in a thin line, they tremble.

"She looks like me," he reasons.

"I have a type," I answer him, turning to face the kitchen counter and giving him nothing but my back. I reach for my tea, desperate to steady myself even though my hands shake. I wish Renee were here. She's helped me keep it together. She reminds me why Robert and I are a bad idea.

7

"We were together right around when—"

"You didn't ask for a baby, and you know … you know she's not yours." My voice breaks at the last little bit. I know deep in my soul she isn't his daughter. She was an accident and a handsome man named Brody is her father. He's the other half of that accident and all I have is a first name, so he's practically a stranger.

"You didn't do a test. You can't know for sure."

"Fine," I say, giving in, "we can do a—"

"No." He's quick to shut down the very thing he just brought up. "We don't need to …" I turn back to face him as he continues, focusing on taking one breath in, then one breath out. "You're going through a lot, and I know … you don't want me to be her father."

I wipe under my eyes, feeling both exhaustion and confusion overwhelming me. "What do you want, Robert?" I ask him, truly wanting an answer.

"Do you want to go to the drive-in this Friday?"

Is he asking me out? I can only stare back at him, not understanding. He can't be serious. I've done everything I can to push this man away since I've come home. I have a full plate and I'm barely holding on. *A date?* He is insane.

"You're a glutton for punishment," is all I can manage as a response.

"Don't say that," he replies with far too much compassion, his brow softening as he tilts his head slightly.

Time slips away, the cash sitting in my palm feeling like it's burning my hand.

"There's not an ounce of desire in me to do anything other than sleep," I answer him honestly. "Can you please just take the money?"

"Mags," he says and his voice is pleading. "You can use that money for a sitter, or—"

"Take the rent, Robert." The second I raise my voice I hunch my shoulders and peek down the hall, then back to the monitor. *Please, please don't wake up, baby girl.*

"I know you're mad," Robert starts and his voice drones on, but I can barely focus.

Yes, I'm mad. More than mad, even. I'm full of resentment that my father screwed over this town and left me to pick up the pieces. I'm upset I couldn't be happy about this pregnancy without knowing how I was going to care for her. I had to hide it from this town for as long as I could so they wouldn't add that on top of the judgment I already had coming my way. Robert changed when he found out my secret. He was fine with me pushing him away until he thought I was pregnant with his baby. He doesn't love me. At least that's what I've told myself for months, reminding myself of that phone call when he threw away what we had for no good reason. It took less than five minutes and then everything was different between us.

It's just a knight in shining armor complex that made him help me.

With the hormones and stress from the pregnancy, I don't need more problems added into the mix. Not to mention the heartbreak of navigating motherhood without my own mother here to teach me.

I don't even realize he's done saying whatever it is that he's saying until I recognize a sound that's been absent in this place all day: *silence.*

"It's your money, Robert, please just—"

"I don't want it, Mags." His voice is firm and I snap.

"Take it." I can barely breathe as tears prick the back of my eyes, and I shove the stack of twenties into his chest. "Take it and leave."

With the cash pressed against his front, his hands raise. As I pull away, he has to catch the falling money. "I don't want it."

"I'm not going on a date with you to stay here."

"You don't have to—"

I threaten something I pray won't happen. "If you won't let me pay you, then I'll go somewhere else." I can't afford anywhere else. I know that much and just speaking those words makes me feel sick. Six hundred is a bargain and I'm more than aware of that. "I'm not a whore," I add, barely getting out the words, hating myself. Hating the way Robert thought I'd just be with him again because of the mess I'm in.

I've never felt so low in my life.

"I didn't say you were." Robert's voice is deadpan as I stare into his baby blue eyes, feeling my own itch with a tiredness that hasn't left me in months.

"You didn't have to," I comment sincerely. That gets a reaction from him.

Tossing the money in the trash, Robert holds back from voicing whatever's on his mind. He's good at that, at not responding in anger. He's never called me a name, never yelled at me, but it still hurt when we'd fight, because he could walk away silently. He told me once he didn't want to say something he'd regret. I've said far too much that I regret, and I've barely lived. Still, I can't stand it, knowing he's biting his tongue.

With both of my palms on the counter, I stare at the trash can and listen to him practically storm out, apart from slamming the door. He saves me from that fear. When the door closes with a soft thud, so do my eyes. I'm grateful he didn't slam it and that Bridget is still asleep. Or at least she isn't crying. Anxiously, I pick up the baby monitor on the counter, staring at the black and white image of my baby girl. *Everything happens for a reason*, I remind myself and hear my mother's voice: *it'll be all right, baby girl*. Fresh, warm tears spill out the corners of my eyes, and I can't hold them back this time.

I'm busy whispering the same words to the monitor when the sound of the front door opening forces me to whip around. I don't expect to see an upset Robert striding back in. He rips the lid off the trash can and reaches in, pulling out the cash that's now dirtied with old breast milk and Lord knows what else I threw in there earlier today.

Even with his face scrunched in disgust, he picks out every bill as I stare in shock. "I'm not going to make you pick it out of the trash," he comments, his voice even but low. Wiping under my eyes I watch his face turn sour as he asks, "What the hell is this?"

"Bad milk."

"Bad milk?" I don't know if his question is serious or not as he drops his arm to nearly the bottom of the pail.

"Apparently whatever I'm eating is giving her gas," I confess to him, "because I can't even feed my little girl without hurting her." Watching a baby struggle with pain and knowing it's your fault … that's a part of motherhood I wasn't prepared for. It hurts more than I could have ever imagined.

"You aren't hurting her," he says, consoling me the second the admission leaves my lips, and I can't stand the look in his eyes or the comfort in his voice, so I turn away. "You're a good mom," he tells me as I do everything I can to keep my composure. I don't know what made him come back in, but I wouldn't have ever guessed he'd come back to clean the money he threw in the trash.

He moves to the sink and I watch his broad shoulders flex as Robert washes the bills, rinsing off the old pumped milk I had to throw away. The faucet squeaks as he shuts it off, the cash laying on a paper towel to dry. With a palm on either side of the sink, his tall form hunches over.

"I don't want to fight, Mags." Hearing him say my name and then noting the pain in his voice does something to me. Misery loves company but my God when it gets what it's after, it calls on regret to save its soul.

"I'm sorry," I tell him and I mean it. I don't know what I'm doing; all I know is that everything feels heavy and like I can't hold it up. The trembling of my shoulders as I let out a heavy sob is lessened when Robert wraps his arms around me.

Rocking me gently, he kisses the top of my head and I wish he wouldn't. Because everything in me wants to lean against him and rest.

"I'm not going to take it," he says.

"Then don't kiss me. Please. Stop helping me."

"You need help, though," he states matter-of-factly. I've lost everything in the last year, including my pride.

With a shuddering breath I push away from him, upset that I've sunk so low. I don't recognize who I am and I even hate myself a little.

The baby monitor flares to life with a wail from my

baby girl and it's all I can do to ask Robert to leave. To let me be so I can go back to her.

"I'll get her," he tells me and then leaves me standing there to let his words sink in. I'm so tired, I can barely comprehend what he's said. I've been by myself all day with her and there's never a break.

I didn't know it'd be this hard.

I listen to his steady strides down the hall. I hear him tell my baby girl to hush and go back to sleep as if he's done it a million times before. She calms down in his arms as he sways her back and forth, patting her bottom and shushing gently. With the baby monitor in my hand, I watch him comfort my daughter better than I have all day and it dims any anger I have toward him for starting the fall of dominoes that led to this point.

When she stops crying, it's peaceful for a moment and I'm grateful. I'm so grateful that every wall I've put up comes crashing down.

CHAPTER
One

Magnolia

Present day

G UILT DOESN'T MIX WELL WITH MORNING coffee. Even still, I gulp down the French vanilla and pretend everything's easy to swallow. The regrets, the uncertainties … all of it.

"Couldn't sleep?" Renee questions and startles me, dragging her feet along the floor as she slowly shuffles into the kitchen. A bit of mascara from yesterday lingers under her eyes and she rubs it away, yawning as she does.

"Barely," I comment, rubbing the tiredness from under my eyes as well. Just seeing her eases the tension that's wreaked havoc on every fiber of me since last night when Robert pulled out that velvet box. "I didn't expect you to be up so early."

"Yeah, well, the curtains in your bedroom suck." Humor traces each of her words and picks up her lips.

Her amethyst silk pajamas have an expensive feel and look out of place in my modest townhouse kitchen. Moving my glance to the worn, baggy tee I use as a nightgown, I note how at odds our wardrobes are. I know I could match her with any number of dainty nighties I have tucked in the bottom drawer of my dresser, but last night I needed comfort. So I turned to an old sleep shirt I used to wear in college. Robert's seen me in this shirt plenty over the years. He's stripped it from me and left it a puddle of cloth on the floor next to my bed half a dozen times … and just that thought brings my mood down even farther.

A loud yawn from Renee, which if I had to guess, I'd say was exaggerated, pulls me from my thoughts. Grabbing the coffeepot and pouring herself a cup in her favorite mug of mine, a rose gold number that says "Manifest It" on the front, Renee repeats her question. "So, couldn't sleep?"

"You were hogging the bed," I rebut weakly, letting the playfulness come out more than giving a serious answer. An asymmetric smile pulls at my lips, but the tension still wrestles inside of me and I can't hide that from Renee. Her raised eyebrow tells me as much.

She doesn't push and I turn my back to her, opening the cabinet in search of a bowl so I can pour myself cereal.

Her spoon tinks as she stirs in creamer. Renee tells me I'm the one who steals the covers and as the tiny spheres of sugary sweet morsels fill the ceramic bowl, she adds that her staying over has never stopped me from sleeping before. The cereal box hits the counter with a dull thud and a beat passes in silence as my hunger for anything at all leaves me.

"You're sad about Robert?" Renee asks as I leave the bowl behind me, opting instead for an empty stomach and more caffeine. *The breakfast of champions.*

I could barely speak last night when I got home. It's hard to explain how difficult it is to look into the eyes of one of your best friends and tell him you don't accept his marriage proposal. It was more than a bruised ego that stared back at me from his baby blues. He was devastated … and I did that to him.

"I just feel guilty," I confess into my coffee and blow away the steady steam before taking another sip and then another. I have to tilt the cup nearly all the way back to get the last few drops. I love Robert and I always will. And he loves me; I know he does.

"Here." Renee gestures with the pot, offering to fill up my cup and I meet her halfway. "You shouldn't feel guilty," she tells me like I don't deserve to feel like crap for putting him through that last night.

"I've never turned down a proposal before, but I'm pretty sure that's supposed to come with a few negative feelings." I can feel my eyes roll, which is better than pricking with tears.

Renee snorts. "Yeah, on his part."

Staring at Renee, her hair already brushed and looking like silk compared to my mess of a bun, I wish she understood.

"He was talking about leaving and starting fresh."

We can start over. Us and Bridget. If you're ready for more, I want it with you. I want to be with you forever, Mags.

Remembering his confession makes me grip the counter behind me to remain upright. The words were spoken with raw vulnerability and I couldn't stop him until he pulled out the box.

"I wish you had been there. He sounded desperate, Renee. You should've seen him." Again, Renee scoffs at the idea.

"He wanted to leave Beaufort?" She blinks comically, both hands wrapped around the coffee mug.

"As if I'd want to leave this place. I don't ... I don't know where that came from." Last night, I saw the same man who stood in front of me only a few feet away from where I am now, begging me to let him help. And just like back then, I told him no.

"You told him no, you're never leaving this place, right?"

"Of course I did." The mug clinks as I set it down on the counter. "I don't know how he could even think of leaving. This is our home." Renee's eyebrow quirks at the use of "our," but she lets it slide, opting to swallow down whatever sarcastic comment was hoping to slip out.

"So Brody comes along and suddenly Robert wants to put down roots." Renee's remark drips with implication.

Brody. Just hearing his name twists my heart.

"I don't want to hurt anyone, but we need to do a paternity test. I get that Robert doesn't want the town talking, but it is what it is."

"The town is already talking."

"What?" Instantly nervous pricks settle down my neck. I hate the rumors and gossip. It's never done a bit of good for me. More importantly, this involves my Bridget. The town gossips can keep my baby girl's name out of their mouths.

"I mean … it's not a bad thing. That rumor started years ago when you came home pregnant."

"Right, so nothing new?" I ask her cautiously. I'm always the last to find out what people are saying.

"Well," Renee begins as she leans against the counter nonchalantly, "you used to just be a ho, but now you're a nice ho with the cutest little toddler and an 'interesting' love life."

I chuckle and when I do, Renee bursts out laughing. It's all just ridiculous. It used to get to me and, judging by my initial reaction, I still have a bit of PTSD from it, but the labels they hurl at me don't do a thing to knock me for a loop.

A broad smile spreads across my face and I can't help it. "Well, they're right that little Bridgey is the cutest."

"Seriously, though, it's a good thing you told him no." Renee doesn't get it. He loved me when I didn't even like the person I was. My smile dims. They can label me with a scarlet letter and all if they want; that doesn't matter. What does matter, though, is that someone is going to get hurt. I can't let it be my daughter. The seriousness of it all feels like it's drowning me.

"And what if we get the test and he's the father?" I say the question I'm thinking out loud. "I just told him no and he very well may be her father."

"Seriously?"

"It's possible and you know it is."

"When it comes to you marrying and settling down, it doesn't matter who the biological father is." Renee's answer is firm.

"I know that," I say, agreeing with her. "It just makes things awkward." *And he's been there for us.* The second bit stays silent on my lips. We've been there for each other for years.

"It's not awkward, it's just ... what it is. It's real," Renee corrects me with a tip of her mug and a raised brow.

"Such a positive spin," I comment dryly, feeling slightly better but I'm still an exhausted ball of anxiousness. How is that combination even possible?

"Just call me Positive Polly."

As the moment ticks by, I finally pop a dry piece of cereal into my mouth, followed by another of the berry red morsels.

"I need ... I need to be able to think straight. I don't understand why I didn't do it sooner. Even the cheek test ... like why did I cancel it?"

"The cheek test?"

"I ordered a swab kit in the mail and then canceled it because I'm a chicken."

"What the hell are you talking about?" she asks, stealing the bowl of cereal for herself, dragging it by its lip across the counter. I guess "cheek test" isn't quite specific enough.

"An at-home kit. For the paternity test."

"Because of Robert," Renee states and I shake my head, denying it.

"It's because I feel almost certain she's Brody's."

"Well, Robert didn't help," she says and bites the inside of her cheek. Like she's holding something else back.

"Why do you hate him so much?" I've never questioned their relationship before. "We were all so close back in high school and after." I would say college days, but Renee never went.

"He broke your heart."

"If I can get over that, you should be able to."

"Yeah, well …" Renee shrugs. "Maybe one day." Sometimes I wish people didn't know all the history between Robert and me. Including Renee. I wish all my mistakes weren't published on every corner of this town.

Clearing my throat, I rest my lower back against the counter like Renee and check the clock. It's after 8:00 a.m. and a Saturday. Of course Bridget would sleep in on the one day where I couldn't get in a single wink.

"Let's get this over with," I say while grabbing my phone from the counter.

"What are you doing?"

"Sending out the most awkward text of my life." The pit of my stomach argues that it's more than awkward.

"What are you texting?"

"That I need them to go and get blood drawn for a paternity test."

"You're texting both of them that?" Renee questions.

"Both men in one chat," I answer her as I press send and then add comically, "like the shameless harlot I am."

That comment gets a laugh and an eye roll from each of us. This town and everyone else can call me whatever names they want. I know who I am, I just don't know what I want or what I'm supposed to do with the curveball life threw at me.

CHAPTER
Two

Robert

ASHER'S GARAGE HAS THIS NOSTALGIC SCENT to it. It's an old airplane hangar from the '80s he and his dad converted to a garage. He saved up all the way back in high school to add all the gear he needed to start his own shop. It smells like oil, hard work and well-used machines.

"Asher," I call out as the gravel crunches beneath my feet at the large entrance. The garage door is up and I know he starts his day the second the sun peeks up from the skyline. I take a long look around the quiet lot, not finding him where he usually is: under the car on the lift right in front of me.

"Heyo," Asher bellows from around the corner and

that's when I spot an ancient hunk of metal. It's an engine that's entirely too large to belong to a car, and it sits just before the door that opens onto a hall leading to more offices and storage.

Asher catches me studying the engine as he makes his entrance, a rag in one hand, cleaning up the wrench in his other.

"Isn't it a beaut?" He takes a moment to nod at it.

"Depends." I meet my friend halfway at the engine. "What is it?"

"For the tractor. I'm thinking it'll pull a cart and we can have hayrides this fall."

An easy smile slips across my face as he slaps the side of the metal behemoth. "I just have to clean it up a bit and we should be good." Asher's a solid guy and a good time to hang out with, always thinking about what he can do for the community. "Hayrides for the kids and then the after-party in the hangar."

My lips kick up into a smirk at the thought of it. "Sounds like a good time to me." The second floor of the hangar has seen a number of parties back in the day. I've missed too many of them recently.

"You going to be here?" he asks me, tossing the used rag in a drum in the corner and grabbing a fresh one to wipe the oil from his hands. He's almost always got black crud somewhere on him while he's here. The citrus aroma of orange from some heavy-duty cleaner he uses fills up the space as I follow him around the interior.

"'Course, why wouldn't I be?"

"I heard you were thinking about eloping with Magnolia up north or something like that." Asher smirks at me. His voice is far too casual for what feels like an assault on my heart. I know it's not intentional. He couldn't hide the humor from his eyes if his life depended on it. It takes me a second longer than it should to fix my expression. "I'm just fucking with you, man." He tosses down the blue rag, this one less filthy than the previous one and his hands somewhat cleaner. The light in his eyes dims when he asks, "You doing all right, though?" He turns his back to lead the way to the register and, right in front of it, dangling sets of keys.

One pair belongs to my car that needed an oil change and a look over.

"Feel like shit."

"Over Magnolia?" he questions with sincerity. Normally I don't like hearing anyone ask about her or talk about her. It's none of their damn business what's going on in Mags's life. When it comes to Asher, though, I know he's asking for good reason.

"I didn't know that's what the word was," I answer and then take in a deep breath. There's no one in this town I owe a damn thing. But Asher, with all the shit that happened over the last four years, I owe him more than anyone knows.

Clearing his throat, he snatches my keys from the pegboard and turns to look over his shoulder, a smile still lingering. "You know it'll change by lunchtime." He adds a wink for good measure.

"Ain't that the truth."

He rattles off a number of things. Something needed replacing, another something had to be ordered, and when it's in he'll give me a call. It's all business for a moment until the cash register closes and he squares his shoulders, facing me and crossing his arms over his chest.

Asher's a backwoods kind of guy. Grew up on motocross and hunting. He's a straight shooter and when he peers back at me, his gaze questioning, I know he's going to pry.

"Heard you were going to that gallery thing, your folks going too?" he comments. His faded blue jeans are smeared with oil on the right side. His polo seems to be new, but it's already fit for the hangar, marred with that same oil up the same side.

"I'll be there, but they're not coming. Pops has backed off a lot recently." Asher nods along, organizing something on the counter into small plastic bins.

"How's your mom?" he asks, his words much more careful than any others.

"The same," I say and I'm quick to change the subject back to the gala Mags is putting on. "Some suits are coming into town and I'm taking them to the event."

"Politics?" he questions, his brow arched. Anything that refers to work of any kind in government is "politics" to him and he never fails to tell me how much he hates it all. Ever since middle school he's told me he prefers anarchy. I don't think he really knows what it means, he's just tired of how slow it can all be.

"Yeah," I answer him and lean back against an old bench. "Wining and dining. You going?"

I have to laugh when his head rears back and he replies, "Hell no." A few seconds later he adds with a broad smile, "I'll be at the after-party, though."

"Where's that?" I question, feeling a bit of ease that I shouldn't trust.

"Supposedly the backyard of the new bar." *Bingo.* I knew it. He's still sniffing around for information about Mags.

Asher could outright ask me what's really on his mind, and if I don't give him what he's after before taking those keys he's got dangling from his fingers, I know he will.

"Oh yeah?" I mimic his stance, crossing my arms over my chest and wait for the questions.

"That new guy ... Griffin. Seems all right," he comments and I'm damn surprised how much my heart races and my body heats. I could've sworn he was going to say Brody. The tension and anxiousness are enough to make me look away from a friend I've known my whole life. Just the idea that Asher holds any opinion of him at all makes me uneasy.

"Yeah, I met him. Looked up him and his friend when they filled out paperwork for the licensing."

"Haven't met that one yet."

"Brody?" My body's rigid and my jaw tight, but somehow I manage to say his name.

"Yeah … I take it you have?" he prompts.

Staring down at the place in the cement floor where I helped him fix a crack a year or two ago, I answer, "He's all right."

Asher stares at me a moment, his gaze drilling holes in the side of my head. "So he's all right?"

It fucking kills me to confess, "I wish I could tell you he's not. Believe me."

His ever-present smile fades as the curiosity and questions settle in the faint laugh lines around his eyes. Like me, he's in his mid-twenties. Asher's a bachelor and a read-between-the-lines kind of man.

"They should be opening soon. It looks like it'll be a fun place."

"Yeah, I reckon it will be." I rub the stubble at my jaw. If I wanted, I could tell this whole town that Brody's not welcome. I could start it right here, right now, with my friend Asher. He's on my side and he's a damn good friend. But if I did that, I'd be a liar and Mags would never forgive me.

"So, you coming then?" Every question seems carefully worded. "To the after-party."

Clearing my throat, I'm equally careful with my response. "Only if I get everyone on board to sign this education budget shift ... and if I'm invited."

Asher nods slowly and seems to bite his tongue. I'm not sure if he wants to spare my feelings but fuck it, I left my heart bleeding on a table last night. There's not much more damage Asher could do.

"You've been dancing around something. Just spit it out." Feeling a tightening in my chest, I force myself to add, more calmly, "You know I'll tell you."

"You really asked her to marry you? Miss Jones said there was a ring box on the table at dinner."

Pinching the bridge of my nose, I nod, my eyes closed. "Yeah, I did."

"And she said no?"

I'm quick to correct him. "She said it's too soon." There's still hope. I may be a fool for holding on to it, but there's still hope.

"How long have you been seeing her?" he asks and I don't know how to answer.

My throat's tight and I shove my hands into my

jacket pockets, looking past the parking lot to the thicket of trees just beyond it. There's a slight chill in the early morning air.

"Really, man? Friends for how long, and you know I know."

"You know what, exactly?" I ask and my question comes out defensively. For a moment I think he knows about it all. Every sordid detail. Even the reason I broke up with her in the first place. I never should have gone against my gut and trusted my father. I knew it was a mistake. Still, it's hard to blame my father, or anyone other than myself. None of what happened next was supposed to happen.

"That you never stopped being sweet on her."

"Yeah, well … yeah. Not much else to say."

"So … is she going to say yes or what? You single or not?"

"It's whatever she wants." Staring off into the trees, I pretend the box in my jacket pocket isn't burning against my palm.

"And if it was up to you?"

"I wouldn't have asked her if I didn't mean it." My tone's harsher than I'd like it to be, my words curter.

"True. I'm sorry to bring it up. I didn't realize …"

"Not your fault. It's not like I told anyone what's between us."

"Your mother?" he questions, once again bringing her up.

"Hell no … No one."

"Not to sound like an ass," Asher starts and I side-eye him, certain he's going to sound exactly like an ass, "but did you tell Magnolia what's between you two?"

I can't help the laugh that leaves me from deep in my chest. "She knows," I say and smile at him, but it's forced. "I thought she knew how much—" The words are cut off, stuck at the back of my throat.

"Well … you know she knows now."

"Of that, I am most definitely aware." Licking my lower lip, I think that's the end of it, but Asher presses on.

"Guess you should've asked her before Mr. Paine showed up, huh? That's his name: Brody Paine?"

His questions answer my own regarding just how much he knows. That blow to the chest I was expecting earlier hits hard. I suppose it was bound to happen eventually.

"Yeah … guess I should have."

CHAPTER
Three

Brody

GRIFFIN'S MUTED LAUGHTER IS AT COMPLETE odds with my wince as I peel off the tape and gauze, ripping out several pieces of hair on my arm along with the tape.

"What are you laughing at?" I ask as we walk down the sidewalk, the sun shining and the breeze carrying that hint of salt I love so much. The weather and this town are straight from the pages of a storybook, but there's not a single thing that could brighten my disposition after this morning.

He finishes his text, nearly tripping on a worn tan brick that's sticking out from the paved sidewalk, and then turns his broad smile toward me. There's a ball of anxiousness that won't quit churning in my stomach, and Griffin knows. He's doing his damnedest to lighten the mood. With my throat going tight at the thought, I ball up the tape and toss it into the nearest trash can on our walk.

"Just something Renee said."

"What's that?"

"Nothing." His grin stays in place although he drops his phone to his side. I have to admit, he's more at ease with Renee than I've ever seen him with a woman.

The thought of Renee inherently reminds me of my own dilemma.

That incessant insecurity stirs in my chest at his answer. I imagine they're talking about us. About Mags, me, Bridget … and unfortunately, Robert. I won't be all right until I get the results back from the blood test. Two to seven business days. That's two to seven days too long, if you ask me.

"What's going on with you two?" The question leaves me as we reach the front entrance of our bar. I can't help the faint smile on my face, even if my nerves are eating me from the inside out. It's all coming together faster than I thought. Griffin wasn't lying when he said as soon as the paperwork was done that we'd be ready to go within weeks.

"Nothing." Griffin sobers up slightly at my questioning, slipping his phone into the back pocket of his jeans. "Yet," he adds and tilts his head, gesturing to the sign that's ready to be placed front and center of the building: Iron Brewery. It's wrought iron with a rustic feel and we're only waiting for a guy named Asher to come down and install it. According to the town, he's the one with the equipment to do any of this.

"Nothing?" I shoot him a grin at the ridiculousness of that statement. Running his hand through his hair, Griffin clears his throat and doubles down. "I'm telling you. There's nothing going on."

I stare him down, from his work boots that match mine, bought after the unfortunate incident of Griffin stepping on a rogue nail in his flip-flops, all the way up his faded blue jeans to his simple tee before meeting his gaze. "Yeah, okay." My response drips with sarcasm.

His only response is to shrug before opening the doors to our joint business.

"Shouldn't lie to your business partner," I mock scold him.

"I swear to you, nothing's going on," he repeats and I shake it off. There's chemistry between them and if he doesn't see it, he's blind.

Judging by his smile and how fast he reaches for his phone when it goes off again, so fast the door nearly closes and smacks him in the face, he's not blind at all. Catching the door before it can deliver him the karma he has coming for fibbing, I stare at his phone with my brows raised, the question not needing to be spoken when he finally looks up from whatever she's sent him.

His expression is hilarious, like a kid caught with his whole arm in a cookie jar, sitting on the floor with crumbs scattered about his face. "I just think she's a cool chick."

I don't buy that response for a second, but whatever he wants to tell me is just fine. I have my own shit to worry about. Shrugging like he did and wearing a hint of a smile, I let it go. The second I do, though … I'm brought back to that gut-wrenching pull. All I can think every single time there's a second that passes without my mind being occupied is that I might be a father. That cute little girl with curly hair … she might be mine.

I could be a father. Right now. To a child I've never even met.

My stomach drops again and so do all of the positive feelings that should come to me as I take in the bar. The flooring's in place, the lights are being hung and the smell of fresh paint lingers in the air. All that can be heard are the intermittent sounds of power tools mingling with the country music the crew has playing in the background. The old radio with a swipe of paint across it is covered in a fine layer of sawdust.

I expect Griffin to go through the rundown of our checklists like he's done every morning. Every day we do a hundred things, and yet the to-do list has been longer and longer the closer we get to the opening.

That's not what he asks, though. "Did Mags answer you?"

My brow lifts at his decision to use Robert's nickname to refer to Magnolia. I know damn well he calls her that. "You calling her Mags now?"

"Better than Rose," he jokes back and that sickening apprehension in the pit of my stomach churns again.

"Real funny." The memory of that prick sitting across from me, threatening to take her away like he had that power, still pisses me off. Rolling back my shoulders, I try to get out any of the tension; it doesn't work, though.

"So he was her first love. And he might think he has some claim to her, but she told him no," Griffin reminds me.

"Right," I answer him and inhale a deep breath. It's cut short by the door swinging open behind us.

"Hey now." A voice I haven't heard before that has a slight twang to it comes from behind us. I greet the man, who looks to be about our age and wearing a black shirt, board shorts and a worn pair of flip-flops, with a nod. His smile is contagious, though, as he reaches out for a handshake, meeting my gaze and then Griffin's.

"Finally get to meet the newcomers in town," he

comments and then answers my unspoken question. "I'm Asher."

"Oh, perfect." Griffin claps once. "You've got everything you need to hang it?"

Asher nods, and before he can answer someone calls out his name behind us and he waves. Glancing over my shoulder, a few guys call out a greeting to the town handyman.

"Went to school together," Asher explains, leaning forward.

"Seems like everyone went to school together around here," I joke.

"Well, there is only one high school." His answer is deadpan.

"Right, right."

"I just wanted to come in and let you guys know me and my buddy are going to come 'round tonight and get that sign up. Shouldn't be too late, maybe around five at the latest."

Resisting the urge to check my phone, I'm almost certain it's not even ten yet.

"That works for us," I tell him. "Whenever is good for you."

"You guys be around then?" he asks and Griffin takes over the conversation. As I'm slipping my hands into my pockets, letting the fact sink in that this is really happening, that this dream we thought up together years ago is finally coming to fruition, another crew member walks in. I know him decently now since he and his brother Ben are talkers. Tom gives Asher a manly slap on his shoulder as he walks by, interrupting the conversation.

Asher returns the friendly smile and asks how Tom's sister is doing.

It's an easy, natural exchange for only a moment, but it's so much more than that. The realization dawns on me that this could be my life. A small town where everyone knows everyone. Where life is seemingly easy and simple, yet tangled in the social aspects.

It's different from the suburbs I came from and where I grew up. It's hard to describe the feeling that brews inside of me. Shuffling my feet, I can only half listen to the rest of the conversation, my mind occupied with thoughts of a little girl everyone here knows better than I do.

And the woman who raised her on her own. I didn't think that I cared what anyone had to say, but a protective part of me has its hackles raised and wants to know everything that's ever been whispered in this town about both of them.

Including the parts that contain information about Robert.

This could be my new life … or not. For a moment, a thought wriggles into the crevices of my mind: What if it doesn't work out with Magnolia? The permanence of it all steals my complete attention and I don't even realize Asher's gone until Griffin tells me to snap out of it.

"Shit." The word is muttered under my breath. Running a hand down my face, I apologize.

"It's fine. You've got a lot on your mind."

Taking in a deep breath and forcing myself to exhale slowly, I stare at the front doors to the bar before agreeing with him.

My gaze is snapped back to him when he asks, "Did you tell your mom?"

"And give her a heart attack?" *Is he fucking crazy?* "No I did not."

My reaction only makes Griffin's smile broader. "Probably best to wait."

"Yeah," I say and it's the only word I can give him.

"When do you find out again?"

"Up to seven days." That's the third time I've told him so far today. I bite back the thought that nearly slipped out unbidden: I hope she's mine. I don't know where it came from, and the thought is scary as hell.

"I'll wait to know for sure before I tell her anything," I tell Griffin and he nods agreeably.

"Fair enough." Then he adds, "You never did answer my question."

"What's that?"

"Did Mags text you back?"

I ignore the hairs raised at the back of my neck by hearing her nickname … the one Robert used. I can't hear it without thinking about him as he sat across from me at the table.

"Yeah," I say then pull out my phone from my back pocket and bring up the text messages. Me to her: *I'd like to meet her if that's okay.* Her response was immediate, leading me to believe she'd already thought a lot about it: *Come by tomorrow night.*

"You want to come with me tomorrow?" I ask him and Griffin lets out a laugh.

"Renee already invited me."

It takes great effort not to shake my head at his response.

"What if I am her dad?" I ask because I just can't help it. It's all I can think about.

Griffin's response is far too lighthearted for my frustration and impatience in wanting to know the truth. "Well then you lucked out in a way, missing the dirty diapers."

"I didn't plan on this and I'm dying inside not knowing."

"Imagine how she felt." His comment is the most serious tone he's taken today.

"What?"

"You're feeling all sorts of ways right now. Imagine

how Magnolia felt. Not knowing but having to do it all on her own. You can suck it up for a week."

"Well damn."

His hands go up in defense as a crease settles between my brow. "Don't be mad at me," he adds.

"I'm not mad, I'm just lost."

"You'll know soon enough."

If I'm not the father and Robert is ... there's no way I have a chance with her. Scolding myself for sounding like a damn child, I attempt to shut up the voice in the back of my head that keeps thinking: it's not fair.

None of this is supposed to happen this way.

CHAPTER
four

Magnolia

"**Y**OUR WORTHINESS IS NEVER ON THE table," I whisper beneath my breath, my eyes closed and my head tilted back. It's a mantra from some self-help audiobook I listened to years ago. "Your worthiness is never on the table." I think it came from *The Power of Vulnerability* by Brené Brown. I need to search my history and listen to it again. The only thing I took away from it was the saying: *Your worthiness is never on the table.* Promotions and other degrees of success may be, but my worthiness of love, including self-love, never is.

Blowing out a deep breath I open my eyes and state, "My worthiness is never on the table … even if I'm scared." The last bit is whispered as I look back down to Brody's text message where a single line stares back at me. *I'll be there.*

Ignoring the swell of emotions, I take another sip of bottled water and look around the room. With all of these packages coming in for the event this weekend, the gallery is in chaos. Lord help me. With my fingers playing with the ends of my hair, I let out an uneasy sigh at the sight of boxes piled high into tall stacks on either side of the doorway. Martin, a.k.a. my hero on days like these, needs to get in here and manhandle these cardboard suckers to the back. My pathetic semblance of upper body strength has already lost this war and I know we're expecting another dozen or so shipments today and tomorrow.

Everything from the upcycled plates and artsy champagne glasses, to spotlights for the featured artists is packed in those boxes. Every little detail has been carefully considered and for the first time ever, I didn't need approval for these purchases. Typically we have a budget and I make the arrangements, but every bit is cleared by Mandy before I can spend a cent and reserve a darn thing.

"This is all you," Mandy told me with a nod of approval I've been after for years. She has plans to attend as a guest with "fresh eyes," so everything needs to be perfect. It will be. I'm doing everything I can possibly think of to highlight the old, while also celebrating the new and the colorful future ahead. Color is the theme and I'm bringing it in spades.

Checking my phone as it dings in my hand, I receive an alert that a package is delayed. A puff of air leaves me and tousles the strand of hair in front of my face. It's only until tomorrow, according to the update. My anxiousness revs up and I shudder before texting Martin if he knows what time he'll be in so I can figure out my own schedule. Technically it's his day off; he's only coming in to help because I asked. Yet another reason he's my hero.

Before I can hit send, the chime at the front door goes off and I spin around, my dress twirling as I do, already filled with gratitude that he came in early. The greeting of "thank goodness" vanishes at the sight of Robert in faded jeans and a simple black tee.

"Hey," I say then breathe out, and my entire body heats. Partially because he knows that's my favorite look on him. The top bit of his hair is a little messy, completing the good ole boy look he's got today. When he's not in a suit, and laid back like this, it reminds me of when we were younger.

The other part of me is riddled with nerves, and that piece of me has my hands hiding in my dress pockets and my teeth biting down on my bottom lip. I haven't seen or spoken to him since the proposal and paternity test text, respectively. With my heart fluttering I ask, "What are you doing here?"

The second he smiles, everything eases inside of me. His presence is calming, but my heart still races, not wanting comfort and wanting something else instead. Maybe it's a desire for forgiveness that keeps me choked up.

As selfish as it may be, a part of me wants him to tell me he's not upset at all. That everything is all right.

Ever the charming one, he lets his gaze settle on my dress for a moment then comments, "Don't you look beautiful?"

With a hint of warmth rising up my cheeks, I know he made me blush. "Well, thank you," I respond and tuck my hair behind my ear.

"What's all this?" he asks.

"I'm doing inventory for the gala." I add in a lowered voice, not hiding my dread, "There's so much that still has to be done."

"You need help?" he asks as if everything's just fine. As if it's any other day and the last week didn't happen at all.

Staring into Robert's soft blue gaze, the last thing I can even think about is him helping me. The question escapes before I can help myself. "Are we okay?"

All I hear in the back of my head is a voice telling me, "No. Of course we aren't." All I can see is how the cords in his neck strain when his smile turns tight and his gaze drops. He doesn't respond for a long moment, and I know it's because he's doing everything he can not to get emotional.

"Robert … I, um …" The word sorry is lost on my lips when he shushes me, like he knows exactly what's on my mind. "It's okay," he starts. His long strides eat up the distance between us but before he can say another word, the chime goes off again.

I anticipate it being Martin and with my mouth open to greet him in thanks, I peer beyond Robert only to have it instantly close again.

Oh my goodness, I have the worst luck in the entire world.

"Hey there," Brody says to me although his gaze moves from my navy dress and matching flats to Robert, who meets his gaze with his once smiling lips now pressed into a firm, straight line.

"Hey yourself," I answer with a bit less excitement than I aimed for, although my smile stays in place. My throat's tight and dry all of a sudden. *I can't imagine why.* If we were alone, it would be different … it would be easy. Still scary, though, and full of uncertainty. That's the realization I've come to. I'm scared of letting go of Robert, but I'm also scared of what Brody makes me feel.

Tingles race down my arms and the back of my

neck pricks after seeing both of these men in the same room together. Both of them aware I've been with the other one, and both of them having to take a test to see who the father of my child is. Both of them staring at the other with the tension in the room growing.

"What a morning it is," I comment half-heartedly and let out an awkward huff of a laugh before clapping my hands in front of me. Awkwardness is apparently my middle name now. To add insult to injury, I don't think it helped to break the tense mood in the room and now they're both staring at me. All I've got for either of them is a nervous smile.

"I can come back—" Brody starts to say, gesturing to the door although the look in his puppy dog eyes is at complete odds with his offer.

Robert's voice is casual enough as he interrupts Brody. "That'd be great—"

"You don't have to," I say, cutting off Robert without meaning to and then share a look with him before returning my focus to Brody. Speaking over each other only adds to the awkward atmosphere.

"I'm working," I say to remind them both and clear my throat, "but I'm happy to see you two." My nerves rear their ugly heads again and my voice wavers when I tell them, "I wanted to say thank you for going through with …" My hand waves as if there's a gesture for a paternity test. "Thank you both for the … samples." If only

I could summon a hole in the ground to swallow me up in this moment.

"No problem," Brody answers easily and Robert speaks up just as quickly, but seemingly more rushed, "Yeah, no problem." The two men stare at each other a second too long, and yet again all the while I can barely stand to look at either.

"I just … I'm sorry I didn't do it sooner so you'd know." Sincerity threatens to bring on more emotion than I'd like, so I move back to the counter and gather up the invoices and confirmations of everything I'd laid out this morning, pretending I don't feel like every inch of me is on fire with embarrassment. Is that it? I don't even know what I'm feeling because it's all too overwhelming.

Suck it up, buttercup, I nearly mutter out loud as my focus stays on the papers while simultaneously not reading a single one of them. I stack them as if I'm putting them in order, but I haven't a clue what's what as I pile them together.

"Don't apologize. You did everything you could, Mags."

"Yeah …" Brody agrees with Robert's comforting statement and I think he's going to say more, but when I glance up at him, tapping the papers on the counter, he's eyeing Robert.

"I just … whatever you guys decide when you know

is fine by me," I tell them both in earnest, a sense of dread overwhelming me. None of this feels like it's in my hands or my control. I'm at the mercy of test tubes and heavy decisions most people don't have to make.

"What do you mean?" Robert asks and I don't even know where to begin. There has to be a book on how to handle this. I should freaking hide away and read a book rather than go out in public and risk running into these two.

I'm saved by another chime. It's insane how much relief I feel at expecting Martin, who I could easily use as an excuse to end this little meet and greet … but again, a different someone is standing in the doorway.

Renee smiles like the cat that ate the canary. There's far too much joy in her eyes at the sight of my predicament.

"Well … hey now," she says and somehow smiles even wider, "I didn't know there was a party going on."

As the two men look at her, I mouth "help me" and give my bestie a pleading look.

"Hey Renee," Robert greets her, slipping his hands into his pockets. A little bit of life seems drained from him as he takes a step back to form a loose circle among the four of us. His gaze meets mine and the hint of a smile doesn't reach his eyes. Whatever he came in here for is long gone.

"Where's Griffin?" Renee asks Brody.

Brody motions over his shoulder with his thumb and says, "He's just down the street if you want to swing by." He glances back at me with an asymmetric smile, obviously adding an invitation for me to join as well, "We're doing a few taste tests today, and I wanted to invite you for lunch if you're free?"

Robert's silent and my heart drops when Renee carries on with Brody, both of them excluding Robert. A new kind of tension takes over. It's just not a good feeling. It's a heaviness in my heart for him.

"Are you guys looking for bartenders for Saturday and the after-party?" Renee asks Brody. I was wondering if she was going to apply at their bar or not. There's something going on between her and Griffin so I'm not so sure it's a good idea, but she hasn't asked me for my opinion, so I've kept my mouth shut.

"Yeah, I think," Brody answers and unexpectedly he turns his attention to the other man in the room.

"You coming, Robert?" Brody questions in a friendly way and a hint of hope lights inside of me.

With his brow raised slightly, Robert lets a second pass before responding, "Depends on if I'm invited."

It's not until Brody answers "Sure," that I let out a breath I didn't know I was holding.

"I came by to see if you wanted to do lunch," Renee says, breaking up the uneasy moment. "If you gentlemen don't mind me stealing Magnolia for a bit."

The chime goes off and I'm nearly scared to look and see who it is that has joined this gathering. Martin's voice is heard before he comes into view. "You weren't joking that the front was becoming a warehouse, were you?" The elderly gentleman's donned his everyday overalls and brown work boots. He barely wears anything else.

"Morning, Martin." Robert greets him with a smile.

"Nearly noon now. How's your day going?" Once the question leaves him, Martin steps forward and both Brody and Renee come into view for him, previously obstructed by the stacks of boxes.

The old man can't hide his shock judging by his raised brow and the tilt of his head that forces the glasses to slip down his nose just slightly. "Well now, I hope you all aren't here for these boxes." There's a slight hint of humor in his tone, but more than that, he sounds concerned as he glances toward me. My cheeks flare with heat at the realization that he's certainly heard the rumors. I'm sure a handful of those rumors are true too.

"Hi Martin, I'm Brody." His outstretched hand is met by Martin's. "Nice to meet you."

"Same to you." I don't know why, but the seemingly innocent interaction makes me nervous. Like there's a whole lot riding on such a simple thing as an introduction.

"Apparently Mags is a popular lady," Renee jokes lightheartedly. "We were just gathering her for lunch. Do you want us to bring anything back?"

She doesn't tell him where we're headed. No doubt Charlie's Bar and Grill since it's only a five-minute walk from here.

"Just ate," he responds with a shake of his head.

I'm quick to bring back professionalism, offering to help, but Martin cuts me off. Thank goodness. My arms are already sore from the handful of boxes I've gathered myself and organized in the back.

"Don't worry about the boxes, I've got them. You want them any certain way?"

"Just in the back for now, please."

"You need help?" Robert offers. There's not a smile in sight and that now far too familiar ache comes back. I can't deny it hurts seeing him like this, and I don't know if it's hitting him harder since I denied his proposal or if it's all in my head.

Martin refuses. "Nope. Don't take my only work-out away from me, son."

"All right then." Robert nods and takes his leave. "You guys have a good time. I'm going to head out."

"Did you need something?" I ask him in front of the audience; I know darn well he didn't just stop by. There's always a reason, and he was going to say something before Brody joined us.

He gives me a tight smile that doesn't reach his eyes. "I'll talk to you about it another time?"

"Yeah, okay." My heart sinks slowly but assuredly as he leaves the gallery, the chime bidding him a farewell.

"We're still on for tonight?" Brody asks the moment Robert is gone and the air is different between us. The heaviness of everything takes its toll on my heart as it skips in my chest, bucking against the reins holding it back.

"Yeah," I answer him and thankfully Renee takes over, asking about Saturday once again.

CHAPTER
five

Magnolia

THERE'S A SAYING ABOUT NOT BEING ABLE TO have your cake and eat it too. It keeps coming to mind when I think about Brody and Robert, but it's not serious enough. It's not cake, it's my best friend. It's not some delicious treat, it's the father of my baby girl.

Maybe there's a different version for more serious affairs but if there is, I haven't heard it. Perhaps a single sentence is just not good enough for matters that destroy the heart.

The sight of the six chocolate cupcakes I bought from Melissa's Sweets brings the saying to the fore-front of my thoughts once again. But you can have half a dozen cupcakes on the kitchen counter and eat some while still having some left over. Did anyone make a saying about that?

"I think I've had too much coffee." The comment leaves me without my conscious consent at the ridiculous thought as I stare down at my hand that's shaking gently before grabbing it with the other.

"Why?" Renee's tone is upbeat and accompanied by the purr of the stuffed kitten in Bridget's hand. The pink plush animal, dubbed "Kitty," is always within a foot of my little girl. That toy and Bridget's knitted cream blanket that's seen better days are the two items in the house I have multiples of … just in case she ever loses them. I'm certain she'd know the difference if that day comes again—it only happened once when she was two—but I have the best excuse already prepared: they took a bath without you, and now they're all fresh and clean.

Cat noises interrupt our conversation and for a moment I forget what I said and what I asked. Oh yeah, my unhealthy caffeine addiction.

"'Cause my heart is all pitter-patter," I answer and then add, "Either that or it's all emotionally exhausting." My cheeks puff up as I blow out a sigh.

Bridget runs off with Kitty, her hair now in a simple ponytail thanks to Renee. It sways left and right as she hides away behind the sofa.

"Well, it makes sense that you're nervous," Renee

tells me as I stack the cupcakes on the tiered tray I got forever ago but have only used once.

The pale pink doesn't match anything else, but it went perfectly with Bridget's birthday decorations back then.

"Nervous is an understatement." I can barely think straight. "I'm surprised I didn't burn the toast."

"Just think of it as … a boyfriend meeting her."

"That doesn't really help." I speak the words slowly, not sure how to explain the bundle of nerves running through me. "She's never met anyone I've dated."

"'Cause you've never really seen anyone," Renee adds and I bite my inner cheek rather than correcting her and reminding her of Robert. He doesn't count. He's always been here and I didn't have to introduce him. Just thinking of him forces my hands to go cold and I shake them out. There's a war brewing inside of me and … well, I'm a mess because of it.

"Mommy," Bridget cries out, rushing back into the kitchen. "Kitty," she says, explaining the situation with a single word and motioning to the bump of hair that's come loose from her ponytail. The plush animal is held in one hand, with a toy mirror in the other.

"Did Kitty do that?" Renee asks her and is met with a curt nod. Renee's grin is comical and it takes everything in me not to laugh when Bridget glances up at me. I bend down to fix it for her.

"Is that better?" I give Bridget a kiss on her cheek as she looks into her Snow White mirror. "Love it," she squeals and claps her hands before racing off.

"I mean, who could possibly not love that little princess?"

Bridget is literally dressed in a princess gown, complete with fake plastic heels. All her choice, and who am I to object?

"It's not about him loving her ... or her liking him. I don't know." Shaking my head, I note how many times I've tried to gather my thoughts. "It just feels so permanent and like I can't go back."

I'm scared. That's the raw truth of it. All of this is new, and so much is out of my control, with more than I care for at stake. Pulling my own hair back, I take in a steadying breath and let the cool air from the open window hit my nape.

"You look tired." Sympathy clings to Renee's comment. Ever since the unfortunate gathering today, Renee's been glued to my side. She may have enjoyed the uncomfortable moment when she first saw Brody and Robert with me at the gallery, but the moment they were gone, I broke down.

It's not a joke or something to laugh at. It feels like my life is being ripped up into tiny pieces and glued back together in some other order and I don't have control over it. It's stressful and I'm stressed.

"You think more concealer will help?" I half kid, although I'm also serious.

"Nah," she says then shakes her head and catches a stray ball that flies into the room. I plaster a smile on my face in response to my daughter's shriek of delight from the catch. "Thought you could pull a fast one, huh?" Renee stands up, pushing back the barstool at the kitchen island and it drags across the floor. Bridget's pulling out her toys in the living room. It was spotless ten minutes ago.

If I cleaned it all up now, I'd just have to clean it all up again in ten minutes. While Renee plays with Bridget, I check on dinner and then glance at the clock again. I swear I look at that digital clock on the oven every five minutes on the dot. It's almost five thirty, the time he said he'd be here.

Well, he and Griffin. Thank goodness for Renee for thinking of that.

When Renee comes back in, I bombard her with the question that keeps rolling around in the back of my head. "You sure I shouldn't have waited?"

"He's just a friend coming over for dinner," Renee reminds me for at least the fourth time since we've been home.

"Right, just a friend." Wiping my sweaty palms down the sides of my navy dress, I do everything I can to calm down, but the ring at the doorbell halts any progress.

"I'll get it," Renee offers, practically standing up the second she sits down, but I stop her.

"I can get it," I tell her and then swallow. "I've got it." I don't know if the last bit was more for her sake or mine.

"Mommy's friends are here," Renee tells Bridget, and I can practically see the smile on her face although my back is to them as I open the door.

It's not at all dark outside, although the sun will start to set soon. The warm hues of the fall sky make the perfect backdrop as I'm caught in Brody's blue eyes.

It's the first time I've seen him in a collared shirt and slacks.

"Hey," I say to greet him and then bite down on my bottom lip as a smile takes over. It doesn't last for long as I blush and tuck a lock of my hair behind my ear.

"Hey yourself." His deep baritone voice is soothing and his charming smile lights something inside of me, something that's comforting. It's as soft as warm blankets in the morning begging me to stay nestled within them rather than start the day. "I got these for you."

He holds out a bouquet of sunflowers, pink and yellow roses, and some sort of white flowers. The plastic around them crinkles and the pink ribbon blows in the gentle breeze that brings the blossoming scents to the tip of my nose.

"They're beautiful." Taking them in both hands, I thank him, shyly looking between him and the bouquet.

I don't even notice Griffin until he asks, "You mind if we come in?"

"Oh, of course." Feeling slightly foolish and letting out a soft laugh, I step back to let them inside. "Come on in." It doesn't escape my mind that Brody's been here before, but not like this.

I catch Renee's look and she smiles at the sight of the flowers. The kind of smug smile that speaks, "not bad."

"Let me just put these in water," I say, feeling all those nerves that left a moment ago come flooding back as Bridget yells out, "Hello!"

With a pounding in my chest, I get ready for the introduction, but the words don't quite come out. It's as if they're just as nervous as I am.

"Oh my goodness," Griffin says and stares at Bridget who's got the ball raised above her head, ready to aim and fire. He looks over at Brody and me still by the door, holding on to the bouquet in my hands for dear life. With wide eyes Griffin looks between Bridget and me then says, "You didn't tell me there was a princess here." He nearly whispers the confession and a simper breaks out across my face.

Renee tsks and says, "I can't believe you didn't know royalty lives here." Griffin's amused expression shifts to one more charming as he takes in Renee. He doesn't fail to notice she's opted for a summer dress for tonight. Renee asked to borrow one from my closet, saying she should wear a dress since I was wearing one too, but I'm certain her decision had nothing at all to do with me. Before he has a chance to finish his "You look—" sentiment, Renee cuts in, a saturated shade of red climbing up her cheeks.

"Princess, meet Mr. Griffin and his friend Brody."

My heart ticks slowly but Bridget doesn't miss a beat, doing what I presume is a curtsy and then flailing her little arms, chucking the ball at Griffin and just barely hitting his shin after a bounce.

A beep from the stove prompts me to move from where my feet seem to have been cemented into the floorboard.

"Dinner?" Brody questions and I offer him a small smile with a nod as I close the front door and rush over to the stove. A single press to the timer button silences it as I call out, "I hope you like lasagna." The oven door opens, revealing a not quite ready top layer of a recipe I found years ago and never stopped loving. I breathe in the aroma as I set the timer for another fifteen minutes.

"I love lasagna," he comments and hearing that word on his lips turns my heartstrings into a fiddle.

The pot holder on the counter becomes my shield to defend against his charm as I pick it up and lean against the kitchen island. Renee has her normal seat in the living room; I can see her over the pass-through window that separates the two rooms. I can't see Griffin, though, who's pretending to be frightened of Kitty and hiding behind the sofa.

Renee may say there's nothing going on, but from where I stand, the two of them are head over heels for each other.

Taking a nervous peek, I watch Brody follow Bridget's path as she plays in the other room. My heart flutters helplessly at his smile in response to the laughter Bridget lets out when Griffin jumps up and lets her chase him around the sofa.

"She's tall," Brody comments before looking at me, and my gaze goes down to the mitt in my hand. As if I wasn't just staring at him, wondering a million thoughts and letting a million more slip by.

"She's a little under average but then again, so am I," I admit to him and remember those early days when she was so low on the charts and gaining weight was difficult. I bite my tongue, trying to find the right balance and wanting to keep things light. All the while, my throat is tight with emotions.

"Well, taller than I thought a three-year-old would

be," he answers easily, still staying back in the kitchen and watching her.

There's a constant soft expression on his face and a spark in his eyes that signals awe.

"What does she like?"

He's just a friend asking, I tell myself. Just a friend. I don't know why it feels like the weight of the world is hanging on the end of whatever answer I'll give him. I've never wanted a soul to approve of my daughter. If someone doesn't love her, they can rot for all I care. She's everything that's good and pure in this world and if they don't want her smiles, it's their loss.

But I want him to like her. I want him to know how perfect she is. Even through the tantrums and ev-er-changing phases that kept me up all hours of the night when she was a baby, she's perfect.

Turning my back to him so he can't see my nervous expression, I open the cabinet and reach for the nicer plates on the highest shelf. I have to stand on my tip-py-toes. It's not fine china like my grandmother used to have. They are a pretty shade of blue, though, and they match the tablecloth I set. Even though I'm fully aware it'll have to be washed tonight and potentially end up stained depending on whether or not Bridget's place mat will remain on the table.

"What she likes changes every month. Sometimes it's bugs and pillow forts." I smile remembering how her face scrunched up last month learning about how a caterpillar really turns into a butterfly. Apparently cocoons are *gross*. "The next month it's soccer and bath bombs."

"Does she like sailing?" he questions as I set the plates down on the counter, listening to them clatter. He still hasn't moved. He suggests, "I could take you guys out."

"We've been to the beach, but not out beyond that."

"Why not?"

"We don't have a boat," I answer him and check on the golden-brown top layer of the pasta dish.

"Well, I do," he states confidently, slipping his hands into the pockets on his slacks and smiling back at me. "If you wanted to do something like that." He glances back at Bridget, and that same soft expression slips back into place. I swear my heart melts in that moment, and it's not from the heat of the oven.

"If you think she'd like it, that is," he adds when I don't respond right away, and I note how easy this all is with him. He doesn't wait for an answer as he tells me they have smaller life jackets for kids and then breaks into a story about his grandfather and the Power Rangers life jacket his grandparents got him back in the day.

"I got into trouble for taking it off while the boat was still in dock," he says and grins at the memory.

"That's your mom's dad?" I ask him and he nods,

then tells me all about his family. That's something I don't have anymore. All I have left of my mother is her watch and the memories. A family is something I could never give Bridget on my own. I'm engrossed in the story he tells without glancing at me, still watching Bridget.

I hadn't realized exactly why he scared me until this moment. New love is dangerous and I'm so very aware I'm falling for him. If I'm honest with myself, I've already fallen and there's no going back.

CHAPTER
Six

Brody

"I FEEL LIKE ..." GRIFFIN SETS HIS FORK DOWN before finishing his thought and it clinks on his now empty plate. His brow is pinched as he stares down to the end of the dining room table. The sun's set since we sat down to eat and it seems like the chandelier above the small table is shining like a spotlight on that little girl. "And maybe this is just me," Griffin says, raising his hands in a defensive gesture.

A smirk kicks up the corners of my lips. He's the polite one. My mother made that comment when she first met him. He's lean, nerdy, and polite as they come. But something about the look in his eyes tells me he's about to put his foot in his mouth. Judging by Renee's fork halting midair and her side-eye zeroing in on him, I bet she thinks so too. "It just seems like she shouldn't be allowed near both pasta sauce and any type of cloth whatsoever." Griffin's gaze is locked on the subject at hand, Bridget. She has one hand holding a chunk of pasta to her fork, and then she uses those chubby little fingers to shovel bite-size pieces of lasagna into her mouth as if finishing first is a competition.

The smile that grows on Magnolia's face is contagious. Even if she is attempting to hide it behind her glass of red wine, which is barely even a glass compared to what Renee poured the rest of us.

"She's a little lady." Renee's statement is Bridget's defense and it makes her smile this toothy little grin. "And she can use the whole tablecloth as a napkin if she'd like," Renee concludes and Magnolia cocks a brow in quiet protest before stating her opposition: "I think not."

A rough chuckle leaves me, which brings Magnolia's nervous gaze back to me. Ever since we sat down, I haven't been able to say much. All I've done is watched Bridget. Griffin is playing the part of investigator, asking her a hundred questions. I'm damn grateful for Griffin and Renee being here and carrying on the conversation.

Dinner's been easygoing, but there's a stirring of anxiousness inside of me that won't quit. I find myself staring at Bridget and then looking up to catch

Magnolia staring at me. The second we make eye contact, hers lower to her now empty plate.

"She's usually a little neater," Magnolia comments and reaches over with a cloth napkin to wipe her daughter's face. It's more than obvious that she loves her daughter. She's almost careful with her, but it's something more. Defensive, in a way I haven't noticed before. Closed off and protective, like she's resistant to any and maybe even all of this.

We're both walking on eggshells in this uncharted territory and that's fine by me. I'm just grateful to be allowed to join them.

"Besides, the place mat is doing its job," she adds. The traceable letters on the plastic sheet beneath Bridget's plate are covered in smears of red sauce as well.

Griffin purses his lips and focuses on Bridget, who obviously loves all the attention. "I feel like she's the kind of girl who will lick her plate." I've discovered she's bright, but funny. She could be a class clown or a star student; I'm not sure which would win out.

Renee agrees with the licking the plate comment and backs up his statement, saying, "She's done it before."

Bridget smiles wide and nods in agreement.

"She's a smart girl and happy." I don't realize I've spoken out loud until Magnolia's voice chimes in, laced with pride. "She is." She's a mini-Magnolia. A tiny carbon copy. Everything about her, from her manner-isms to her expressions, is reminiscent of her mother.

Magnolia's place is small like my apartment, but I find myself thinking about whether or not we could afford something bigger, or if she'd want me to move in here. Or maybe she'd want to move in with me. I could see myself coming home to them. My imagination is rampant, my thoughts scattered. All of them focused on two very different questions:

What if I'm her father?

What if I'm not, but I don't want to let go of Magnolia?

These are questions that shouldn't be hitting me every five minutes since I've planted my ass in this seat. Every time I think it's way too soon to even think about that, another side of me counters that it's way too late and I've missed too much as it is.

With my throat tight, I'm overwhelmed by it all. "You said the bathroom is down the hall?" I ask Magnolia before I can stop myself. Heat flares its way through me and all I can think is that I'm embarrassed I'm not confident in a damn thing right now.

It's too much in this moment. This little girl changes everything and I am barely keeping myself together.

The second I close the door to the powder blue half bath, I turn the faucet on high and lean my palms against the counter, bracing myself as I hunch over the sink.

Deep breaths in and out keep me still. My chest rises and falls with each one.

I shouldn't be breaking down. I shouldn't be thinking of my grandfather and my mother and how close my family used to be growing up. I don't even know if Bridget's mine or what Magnolia thinks of us being more than a rekindled fling.

I don't have any answers and it's fucking destroying me. "Keep your shit together," I command myself as I lift my gaze to the mirror.

Even still, I can't shake the feeling like everything has changed and that she's my daughter. From deep within the marrow of my bones I feel it: she's my little girl.

Stuffing that thought down, I head back expecting to see everyone right where they were, but that's not the case at all.

Renee's seated with Bridget in her lap, cross-legged on the floor of the living room. They're leaned up against the coffee table with chocolate cupcakes in hand, laser focused on whatever cartoon is on the TV.

The clatter of dishes being washed turns my attention to Magnolia in the kitchen.

Before I can utter a word, Griffin slaps a hand down on the kitchen island to get my attention. "You ready to go?" he asks me. I don't know if ending the night right now is an out for me, or if it's what I'm supposed to do or what Magnolia wants. Griffin locks his eyes with mine and I have never wanted to be a telepath more in my life. He isn't giving me shit, just waiting for an answer.

"You need help?" I offer the only thing I can think, raising my voice to Magnolia so she can hear it over the running water.

Her motions stop and she looks over her shoulder toward me with a dish in hand. When she shakes her head, her wavy blond locks flow down her shoulders. Her blue eyes don't give anything away at all.

"Let me show you out." Leaving the dishwasher open, half-full with the rest of the plates in the sink, Magnolia leads us to the door. Not before offering me a cupcake, though, which Griffin takes two of. He's the one with the sweet tooth, so no doubt he'll eat both of them.

My heart pounds and adrenaline races through me as we walk to the door. I can't help but feel like this has changed everything, and I hope she feels it too. The intensity, but not the pressure for it to go perfectly.

"I had a great time," I tell her as she opens the door.

"See you later, little lady," Griffin comments and Renee jokes back. Something about which one; I can barely hear their conversation as Magnolia plants a quick kiss on my lips.

Far too quick. It was all far too fast. I wish I could go back and live it all over again.

The tension thickens quickly as she backs away and widens the door. The nervous prick at the back of my neck wants me to go to her and not leave, but it's ended far too abruptly. Griffin's tone is upbeat and light as he bids her farewell. "Thanks for dinner, Mags."

"Have a good night, guys ... I'll talk to you soon?" she asks me like it isn't a given.

"I'll text you when we get home."

The second the door is closed, I can't hold it in any longer. "There's no doubt in my mind that little girl is mine," I confess to him just beneath my breath. The crickets chirp around us and the sky's turned black. Speaking the words out loud is what does it. My gaze is hot compared to the warm night, the back of my eyes itching and when Griffin asks me what I've said, I hurry my ass down the steps to my truck. I don't answer him until he asks again as I turn the engine over while he buckles his seatbelt.

"Nothing important," I answer him and stare up at her door. "I don't remember what I said," I lie to him, to keep from crying. He asks me if I'm all right and I shake it off then ask him to turn on the radio.

CHAPTER
Seven

Robert

"I DON'T KNOW WHAT YOU WERE THINKING." My father's voice drones on from behind his desk. I can barely focus on him and his tirade. The deep ache that's etched into my chest refuses to leave. There's no soothing it, only distractions. It's just as it was years ago, back when I lost her the first time.

My father's back is to me as he stares out of the large paned window in his office. Turning to look over his shoulder, he shakes his head in disappointment and then his brow furrows, his attention taken by something in the backyard. The dogs, most likely.

"Marriage," he scoffs. The knife digs in deeper.

There's no doubt now it wasn't just time that Magnolia needed. Swallowing thickly, I rid myself of the image of Brody and the way he looks at her … and the way she stares back at him.

Breathing in deep, I catch a hint of the tobacco that creeps from the humidor in the corner of his old office. "Seriously, Robert—" he continues and I lean back in the wingback chair. My thumb runs over a crack in the curved armrest as I interrupt him and say, "I was thinking I'd like her to marry me."

That gets my father's attention and earns me a stern, narrow gaze that eases just as quickly as it came. As I feel a sickening chill from the memory of the last time I sat in this office, suggesting she marry me, the color drains from my father's face.

He may be a hard old man, but he knows what she means to me. Or at least I thought he did until he called this meeting.

"It wasn't a good look—"

"I don't care how it looked." *It was worth it.* Anything I can do to hold on to her is worth it. However it looks, and however painful it is for her to turn me down.

"And it wouldn't have been appealing even if she'd said yes."

Appealing?

My jaw clenches, the back of my teeth grinding

as I hold in every profane word I desperately want to spew at his opinion. The inclination to show respect is ingrained in me, even if there's not an ounce of it sincerely present.

I don't give a damn how it would have looked. For once, I just wanted her to love me and to know I'd have her forever. As much as the confession wishes to slip out, the deep-seated anguish I harbor keeps the thoughts from running away. She said no for a reason and somewhere in the back of my mind, I knew she would. I know she won't ever choose me again. Accepting that truth is too heavy a burden.

One my father doesn't seem to mind pointing out.

"Well, I think we both knew she wasn't going to say yes."

My knuckles turn white as I grip the armrest and answer him with only a nod.

"Then why go through with it?" My father's exasperation isn't hidden as he opens the window and whistles to get the dogs' attention, scolding them for going into my mother's garden. If the screen weren't there, I have no doubt he would lean out of it.

I used to love being here. Not just in this office, but being home. It used to feel like that ... like a home. Ever since my mother got sick and my father stepped back from work, it's turned into a place of strategy, stale with disappointment.

"Did you even think about what that would do to your career?" There's a hint of desperation, of a father urging his son to make the right choices. Years ago, I listened to that tone and clung to it with everything I had in me. That was before I realized that even if he thought it was right, it didn't mean it was right for me.

"There's a lot at stake in the next five years," he says, finally taking his seat across from me and the dim light casts shadows on his face, making him look older than he is. The long days in the sun and years of smoking certainly didn't do his youth any favors either.

"I am aware," I comment, crossing my ankle over my knee and trying not to think about the state my father's in. Taking care of my mother is practically a full-time job and he's a stubborn man on the verge of losing everything. My mother to Alzheimer's, his career because his time has been dedicated to her ... and then there's me.

"It would look good to have a family. Wouldn't it?" I can't help rebutting. With Magnolia and Bridget ... "We'd make a good-looking family." My voice lowers with the thought and I can't hide the taste of the bitter pill I had to swallow in the last comment. It doesn't go unnoticed by my father, and again the tension increases.

Ever since he told me to break up with Magnolia, things have been tense between us when she's mentioned.

I understand why he did it. There was a scandal concerning her father about to break, and I couldn't be attached to it so early into my political career. I was only twenty-one and had just gotten the internship that would set me on the right track. He was looking out for me, and I didn't know which way the wind was blowing or what to even think. It wasn't supposed to happen the way it did and had the plan worked, she would be my wife. I'd have that beautiful family with my first love. It wasn't supposed to be like this.

It was a temporary breakup. When she came home from college and the scandal had died down, I'd beg her to take me back. I still have fucking nightmares over that phone call. Hearing her voice hitch before she sobbed and being unable to tell her the truth shredded me. Knowing I was knocking over the first domino in a series where each one falling only cemented her hatred for me that much more.

I knew it would hurt, but I didn't even give her a reason. In hindsight, maybe that made it worse. If my father hadn't been in the room, I would have told her it was fake. I'd have made her promise to lie. As it stands, I did what I thought I had to do to protect her. It never should have happened at all. I shouldn't have gambled with the only thing I ever wanted. I'm half a man without her.

"If I could go back, I would." I utter the hard truth I've known since the second I ended that call. When other emotions threaten to take the forefront, I pinch the bridge of my nose as if it's a headache and not regret that makes me do so.

"What you need to be doing is preparing your speech for the presentation on Monday," my father says, diverting the conversation.

He's only told me he was sorry once. I'm sorry every goddamn day of my life. Hurting her was meant to be a small sacrifice and would ultimately lead to saving her. My father promised it was for the best. Her name wouldn't be mentioned if we weren't together.

The papers called wanting a lead, and suggested my relationship with her father involved more than just dating his daughter. The angle of the article was that her father's scheming was a family affair.

It didn't just help me for my father to tell them we weren't together any longer. It was to keep her name free of it all too, or so he said.

She wasn't supposed to come home and bear the

brunt of it. It wasn't supposed to happen this way. Her father is a bastard for dying when he did.

"Show them around town, deliver your speech." My father continues, emphasizing each action with a rap of his knuckles on the hard maple desk. "The next morning, you put that pressure on until they sign the deal."

"I'm aware."

"Good." The single word is a strong indication this meeting is over, so I prepare myself to leave, to deal with everything else. An endless to-do list and emails that can't wait. Unfortunately, my father's tone softens and he asks, "Have you spoken to your mother?

"Have I spoken to her about what?" The hairs on the back of my neck stand up. Four years ago when she was first diagnosed, it was upsetting, but my mother was still my mother. Alzheimer's has a way of stealing people from you. The progression has been slow but sure. The thread in our family has withered away just as much as her memory has. My mother's friends hardly call on her anymore. They don't know how she is these days. No one in this town knows … except for Magnolia. Although she doesn't know the extent of it. Only what I've told her at my weakest moments. My mother was never kind to Mags. The two didn't get along and I know it's because of the way my mom talked to her ... and about her.

"That you asked her to marry you."

"To hell with that. I haven't. No." She barely remembers who Magnolia is anymore. Bridget, though, she remembers.

"She's beside herself."

Guilt worms its way in and I find myself adjusting in the chair uncomfortably.

"I haven't seen her." The guilt eats away at me as my father's eyes gloss over. "What did she say exactly?"

"Mom? I didn't tell her."

Before I can reply to that, my father shakes his head and says, "No, no, no." He takes in a steadying breath before meeting my gaze to clarify, "What did Magnolia say when you asked her?"

Although my father's tone is gentle, my response is anything but. "She said no."

"I thought there was something ... between you two?" His voice is low, his words careful and if I'm not mistaken, there's a hint of loss in his gaze. He clears his throat, casually reaching into a drawer as if this conversation isn't important. It's a telltale sign that he's anxious over my answer.

"She said it was too soon."

"Too soon," he repeats in a huff, as if he doesn't

like the taste of the words. I prepare for more, although nothing else comes but a stack of papers from the drawer landing with a harsh thud on the desk. He aimlessly riffles through them, but doesn't really look at a single one, the corners of his lips decidedly turned down.

"You should come to dinner soon." His suggestion weighs down my already heavy heart. He says that when she's worsened. I wish I could say I didn't know how much worse it could possibly get. Unfortunately, that's not the case.

My first instinct when I finally leave is to tell Magnolia, but for the first time in years I hesitate. With the message waiting to be sent, I know I can't hit that button. It's my burden, not hers. When it comes to Magnolia, I've been selfish for too long.

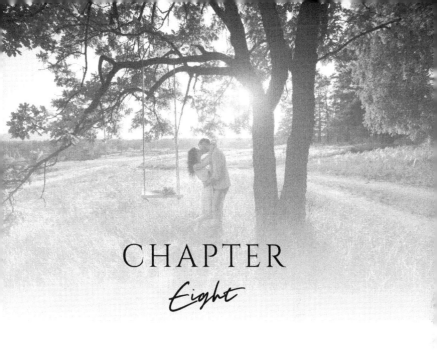

CHAPTER
Eight

Magnolia

Eight years ago

"IS THIS THE ONE?" ROBERT ASKS, A charming smile teasing me as he picks up his pace and rounds the angel oak tree. Ever since I was little, I've loved what people say about this tree. It's the tallest oak in the center of town and I know there are prettier, larger trees in the world, but this one is my favorite.

It's a promise tree.

"This one, right?" he asks again.

"You know it is," I answer Robert as he lets go of my hand. The roots poke out from the ground, and I take a moment to slip off my wedges rather than trip on them.

We have at least a half hour until sunset, but the ambers have already taken over the skyline.

With the straps of my shoes hooked over my left hand, it's harder to adjust my cardigan.

"You cold?"

Even though goosebumps trail along both my arms, I shake my head no. This is exactly what I've dreamed of wearing for this very moment. A flowy white sundress at sunset. Literal dreams have led me here. My heart beats out of rhythm for a moment, taking it all in as I try to swallow down all the restless feelings. This is the start of our happily ever after.

"All right then," he says and Robert's tone tells me he doesn't believe me. He knows me better than anyone, so I'm certain he knows every little thing I'm feeling.

Biting down on my bottom lip, I try to contain the heat that rises in my cheeks. I'm barely breathing when he asks me, "You'll love me forever?" His right hand is touching the tree as I walk closer with bare feet.

"Of course," I answer him easily. There's not a doubt in my mind we'll be together forever. My wavy hair is blown back and I hope he knows how much this means to me. I hope he remembers it forever, because I know I will. To promise to love each other under this tree is all I've wanted to do for the last year.

"Is that all we have to do?" he questions, a light-heartedness in his steps as the sun seems to dim on the

horizon from soft yellow to warm amber. "Just say we will and the tree remembers our promise?"

The boyishness of his grin and the way he cocks his eyebrow proves he's making light of this.

I stop in my tracks just a few feet shy of my first and only love. "Robert," I protest, "stop."

"You have the prettiest pout." He keeps up his teasing as he takes a few steps closer to me and the shade finds us both, hiding us beneath the oak tree from everything and everyone else. I can't help but smile in return when he smiles down at me and steals a quick kiss that I wish lasted for longer.

With my hands in both of his, I tilt up my chin and plead with him, "I'm leaving in just a few weeks and I'm scared things are going to change when college starts. Will you—"

"Never," he says, cutting me off. "Nothing's going to change. I love you, Magnolia Marie Williamson," he states as if he's taking an oath.

My heart skips a beat and a warmth flows through me as he peers down and rests his forehead against mine. He declares, "I love you, and I'll love you forever."

Present day

I truly love this one. My fingers itch to run down the

layered hues of the oil painting. Its texture is achingly lifelike. Everything about it, from the weathered bark, to the dried leaves that fade to an autumn sky, reminds me of something that feels like a long-lost dream. I love it, but at the same time, I hate it. Dropping my hand to my side, I take a step back and forget any pretense of nostalgia. With a steady inhale, I remind myself I'm only emotional because … well, because all hell has broken loose on my life and I darn well should be.

My mantra has changed a bit over the last few weeks. It's always been: I am a strong woman, and I'm raising a strong woman as well. I am worthy and I am doing better with every day.

Now I've added: I might be in love with two men, and that's okay. One I've been in love with all my life, and I can't see a world without him. The other is so new, so delicate and wanted, that it scares me to even think how much he affects me.

I'm just not so sure about that last bit I've tacked on at the end.

"You know I hate raffles, but this is a charity I can stand behind," Mandy says from behind me while she looks at the computer. The clicking and clacking of the keys hasn't stopped since she's come in to check on the upcoming gala. I knew she wouldn't be able to give up full control. Nerves battle within me as she goes down her list.

"It was smart to include it and to really push the artist's wish." The tapping stops for a moment and my lungs stall, praying the typing didn't stop because she's found something she doesn't care for. "It made her that much happier to come."

"Agreed." I step back, adding, "And she'll be less nervous if the conversation is about her passion and not selling the paintings." We've commissioned four from an artist named Ellie Fields. One she's designated just for charity and we'll be donating our end as well. It's for an excellent cause and the publicity we'll garner as a result means it's a win all the way around. I could talk for hours about it, but Mandy's ready to move along. Her perfectly pointed upturned nose directed at me, she questions, "What else?"

"That was all. So long as you're happy with everything." I clear my throat, and move back to the center of the screen, shifting the laptop back to its normal place … back in my custody. "Martin has moved the stock all safely wrapped to the back room, and only the features will stay." She nods along, her cheeks hollowing as she sips her latte.

"Should I come in tomorrow morning?" she asks and I offer her the most confident smile I can muster. "Only if you'd like. I promise this event has my full focus, and it will have every bit of attention it deserves."

"Love is in the details," she says and wags one

perfectly painted pointer in my direction. The scarlet red is *so* her color. Red has always been synonymous with the word *confident* in my mind ever since I read something about the Romans and the color red. Peeking down at my flats, I wish I had time to get my nails done for tomorrow. At least my flats will cover up the evidence that I haven't had them done in months.

But that's because I've been busting my butt. That reminder brings up a renewed sense of pride.

"In twenty-four hours your gallery will be packed, the raffle will support art programs, the artists will livestream on social." I bite down on the very tip of my tongue, holding back the one thing I haven't told Mandy about. In the back of the gallery there's a small slate path to a garden. It's overgrown and far too small for any party guests to venture—but—it's perfect for a painting session from Ellie and with the projector along the back wall, bids can take place during a live event. It's a show and the guests can dictate colors and participate in a way that most will never have an opportunity to do in their lifetime.

Waves of excitement threaten to have me giving away the surprise, but luckily for me, Mandy turns her attention back to the laptop.

As she silently goes through the event listing in the promotional features online, I can only focus on what will be, hopefully, everywhere online the day following our event.

The social media views of live paintings are far higher than anything else we've done on every platform. So the surprise is twofold: another unique art edition, as well as a viral catch for bidders who aren't attending in person but purchased virtual tickets. I want to ride that wave of interest for as long as we can.

"I'm in love with the stained glass fixtures. I must say they're my favorite." Apparently she's gone back to the layout plan for the event. Pride makes me stand a little taller and I have to suppress the giddiness that comes over me.

"They're for sale as well," I tell her. "Everything except for the plates and glasses will be sold at auction, and most items already have bids from the online attendees."

Mandy's sharp gaze narrows on me, but then she gives me a friendly smirk along with her compliment. "You can certainly throw a party."

"Thank you. Hopefully it will be a moneymaker and educational at the same time. We'll have media hype for weeks, if not months, to share as well."

"I know Samantha, the artist flying in from Sacramento," she lowers her voice in a conspiratorial whisper although she doesn't need to. Samantha Pratt is by far the biggest star who will be in attendance as far as I'm concerned. "Sam's impressed, so let's keep her smiling."

"Of course," I say and nod, my hands tucked behind my back and playing with the small ribbon that's tied around the waist of my shift dress. "I spoke with Chandler earlier and the inn already has everyone's welcome baskets and the reception cards."

This time, Mandy positions the laptop facing me, in its normal placement without me touching it. She scoots it there and then turns her attention back to her latte.

"Anyone coming from out of town will be catered to and of course the usuals from in town will aid in wining and dining the way a small town knows how."

Mandy sets down her coffee which now seems empty, judging by the hollow thud of the cardboard cup, and says, "I'm not going to lie, there's been talk and gossip about you." My anxiety ramps up, but not too intensely. Her tone is far too cheery for that comment to be taken negatively. Then she adds, "It's been excellent for ticket sales from people in town," and it all makes sense.

"This town is never out of fodder for good gossip." I smile over my nerves and keep my gaze steady on hers. Although I'd like nothing more than to reach for my bottle of water and take a large gulp, I stay perfectly still in my black and white tailored dress while keeping a straight face. I'm certain my cheeks give me away, stained with red, but my focus is professionalism.

"Well, you are right about that," she says and hums in agreement, although her perfectly plucked brow is far too arched for sincerity.

"I believe everything is all set," I conclude, rocking on my heels.

"You believe?" Her brow somehow arches higher. If she hadn't done it, I wouldn't think it was possible.

"It is. Everything is all set." I'm quick to correct myself and when she smiles broadly, so do I.

"Wonderful, then." She prepares to end the meeting and just then my phone dings and buzzes with a text, distracting me. Thankfully she doesn't notice, already busying herself by gathering her empty coffee cup and slinging her cream vegan leather hobo purse over one shoulder. "I'll be in two hours before."

"I'll be there before then so everything is prepared when you arrive." My assertion earns me a warm smile.

"Thank you, Magnolia." Mandy dismisses me warmly, taking her leave with her keys jingling in her hands.

The second the chime goes off at the front door, I shake out my hands and exhale. Nerves are still making their presence known through every inch of my fingers. With my lips in a perfect O and my eyes closed, I breathe in and then out. I need Renee's freaking whistle that's not a whistle.

If all goes well, I'll be promoted to manager and Mandy will hire another two employees to help me with, and I quote, "whatever it is I need." There's nothing like getting a heads-up via email five minutes before your boss walks through the door to shoot your heart into overdrive.

I could run this place.

Both of my hands reach for the bottle of water as if it'll steady me at the thought. She said that. She said I could run this place.

Again, I breathe out and shake off the nerves by checking every spotlight once again. The last thing I need tonight is poor lighting. I went to college thinking one day I could restore art or maybe be an artist myself. More than a handful of times Renee's suggested I go back and finish my degree. Every time I'm given more responsibility from Mandy, each time I dive more into the business side of the art realm, I stray farther and farther from what I used to want. I crave more of this: the planning, the marketing, and sharing the art I love so much with others who want the same. Life has a funny way of shaping a person and giving them what they never knew they needed.

It isn't until my phone dings again that I remember

I had a text. I'm in my own world far too often these days. Grabbing my phone, I check my messages.

How did it go? Both Renee and Robert sent the same question.

Reading those texts makes me feel like I used to. For a very small moment in time, everything is how it used to be. As I text both of them that it went perfectly, it's just like normal. The everyday ebbs and flows. Until I remember Brody and everything else. It all collides into that bit of familiarity and makes me want to loosen the ribbon around my waist.

The town is talking. I remember what my boss said. I opt to leave that bit out as I fill Renee in with the details, including the bit about Mandy loving the stained glass features.

Give yourself a pat on the back … and a mimosa at lunch, Renee texts back. After texting her *Cheers to that*, I check Robert's message, which steals the smile from me.

I miss you.

I almost tell him something he's said for years. It's the same thing he's told me when I've been low: *I'm right here.* But I delete those words as quickly as I typed them. With my throat tight, I'm blunt in my next message: *Are you mad at me?*

Never, Mags.

I hesitate to text him the truth, but it is the truth and so I do it: *I miss you too.*

As if they heard me, a group thread lights up at the top of my texts.

Don't forget, playdate tonight, Autumn messages all four of us, Renee included. Even though not all of us have kids, we all need each other to help us hold on to sheer sanity in this town.

Part of me thinks I shouldn't be drinking the night before an important event. The other part of me knows I need a drink the night before an important event. A little venting won't hurt either.

I'll be there. Sharon answers first, quickly followed by Renee: *Me too!*

Mags, you'll be there, right?

Unless she's seeing your man, Sharon responds in the group chat before I get a chance to say anything. My heartstrings are pulled in every direction at that. Autumn questions, *Which man?* Before I can even think of clarifying, Renee pipes up in the chat.

Brody's gone for the next two days. He's taking a trip up to his hometown to get some things.

I'll be there. I offer my short response without giving an opinion or insight into the above texts. Not until Sharon asks, *Will he be back for the gala?*

A short *Yeah* does the trick and the chat is filled

with glasses of wine and baby emojis, from the singles and the mamas in the chat, respectively.

One glass of wine and I know I'm going to spill it all tonight.

Breathing out all the pent-up tension yet again, all I can think is: *What the hell am I doing?*

CHAPTER
Nine

Brody

I STILL HAVEN'T TOLD HER, BECAUSE I'M chickenshit. The more my palms sweat along the leather steering wheel, the more I'm convinced I won't be telling my mother anything until I have the results back and I know without a doubt Bridget's my daughter. Maybe there's some kind of telltale genetic sign when a father meets his kid. I don't know. I don't know how to explain it, and that in and of itself is a reason to not breathe a word of it to my mom.

"You can roll down the window if you really want," my mother comments with a hint of humor in her tone. As she pulls back her hair into a braid she adds, "I was only joking when I said it would mess up my hair."

"I'm fine, Mom."

"Then I'm turning on the air," she tells me lightheartedly.

"You don't have to."

"Well, if you aren't hot … are you sweating because you're nervous about something?" she pries. My mother is good at prying, if nothing else.

Thump, my pulse races, not liking where this is going. I've never been a good liar and when it comes to my mom, I haven't gotten away with a single one. This isn't sneaking out or causing a fight at a bar … this is something I'm not ready to talk about.

"I know I told you I wouldn't ask," my mother starts before I can answer her question.

"Then you should probably stop while you're ahead," I offer her with a tilt of my head toward the sign on the side of the road. I'm eager to change the direction of the conversation. "You need to make a pit stop?"

"I'm good if you are," she counters and I find my hands twisting around the steering wheel again.

We've got hours left of her picking away, interrogating me in the guise of asking innocent questions. My gaze shifts to the clock as she turns down the volume on the radio until I can't hear the alternative station anymore. Hours.

"How are you on money?"

That question catches me off guard and as I glance at my mother, I know it's serious because she's not looking at me. Her eyes are focused on the cars ahead of us on the highway. "You've never asked me that before."

"You've never moved and dumped all of your savings into a bar before."

"Fair point." My acknowledgment is barely heard over the hum of the AC, let alone my screaming thoughts.

"So?"

"You don't have to worry about me, Mom."

"Of course I do, I'm your mother." She offers me a pat on the thigh as I drive, and I catch a glimpse of her and note a warm smile along with a happiness in her blue eyes as she adds, "It's in my job description."

Easing back into the driver's seat, a sense of comfort takes over. Partially from the fact that I now have a conversation to eat up time, one that protects Magnolia and Bridget from my mother's prying eye.

"I have a backup plan if the bar struggles at first."

"Does it involve cashing out the trust from your grandfather?"

My mother's a banker. She's as logical as they

come. Not a wanderer or a romantic. She's a numbers and logic kind of woman.

"No. I haven't touched that." I nearly tell her I'm saving it for when I have children but then Bridget's cherubic little face flashes in front of my eyes.

"Well, so what then? Spit it out."

The turn signal ticks as I slip into the left lane for an upcoming off-ramp and gather my thoughts. I have it all written down and I went over it a thousand times already, but still, I know she's going to ask questions I may not have the answer to.

"Liquidating stocks would be first."

"I don't like the sound of that." My mother's disapproval comes complete with a frown.

"I sunk all my cash into the bar, so I don't have much choice. I've got a small place down here, Mom. I'm not spending much, but if it comes down to it, I'll need more cash to keep it afloat."

"And Griffin?" she questions.

"Same with him." In my periphery, I watch her nod and then I add, "We're in this together."

"I know you are," she says and her voice is amiable. "That's why I'm nervous. It's not just a lot of money. It's also business with a friend. And you don't do—"

"You don't do business with family or friends. I know. But this is *our* dream, Mom."

A smirk kicks up my lips when I can practically see her biting her tongue.

"I love you, I love both of you," she says, emphasizing the word *both*, "and I don't want anything to get in the way of your friendship. Especially not money."

The conversation turns easy. She's worried, but she doesn't have to be. Her fingers play with the cuffs of her oversized cream sweater, her nerves showing.

"It's not just a bar, Mom." All of the late-night talks with Griffin back when he was in college and I was backpacking across the country come back to me. I'd send him pictures and ideas, and he'd meet me halfway with more ideas of his own. "We already talked about what would happen if things went south and even though I know he'd hate it and I would too, we signed an agreement."

"And what's that agreement?"

"If profits dip below a certain point, we shut down the bar and rent it out to focus on the retail side with the beer. It makes sense. The easiest ROI even though the ceiling is lower. It's sustainable and renting out the bar would keep those costs flush until we can sell it." Just the thought of doing that makes my blood run cold. The idea of giving our dream to someone else if we can't make it work makes me restless and uneasy.

"You know restaurants and bars are hard, but—" my mother starts.

"But liquor stores survive everywhere," I say, completing her sentence for her, then glance at her with a knowing smile. She's told me that a thousand times. Even though she's questioning my game plan now, she's never failed to support me. "Yes, I know. And Griffin knows too."

A moment passes of quiet contemplation and it's only then that I realize she turned off the radio at some point. My mind drifts to the bar, and to making a family down there. To Magnolia and Bridget. "I'm not planning on failing, though."

My mother seems caught off guard by the determination in my voice, judging by the way she stares at me. She comments just above a murmur, "No one ever does."

While I'm taking in a deep breath, prepared to respond, my mother says, "You know I believe in you two. In all aspects, and you've always been business savvy … I just worry is all."

"Well, when you see it, you'll stop worrying."

"I thought it wasn't ready."

"There's still some plumbing to do and I could use some opinions on décor," I say, offering her the option to help as a peace treaty to stop talking about the "what ifs" if things don't work out. I'm not naïve and I have plans for every outcome. I won't settle for failure, though. And I damn sure don't like talking about any possibility other than living the dream I worked too damn hard for to let slip through my fingers. Doing it there at that bar specifically. That town. Because it's where Magnolia is.

"How's Griffin?" I glance at the clock before replying … hours remaining. More picking. More investigating. I should have turned on the damn radio.

"He's good."

"Does he have a girlfriend?" she questions and I know this is her way of prying into my own love life. Shit.

"I think he might." I offer up gossip about my best friend in lieu of having to tell my mother about Magnolia while I'm trapped in this truck with her for another five hours. We used to do long road trips when I was younger. My grandfather would drive, with my mother in the passenger seat and me in the back. We went to Yosemite and other national parks, baseball stadiums and Niagara Falls.

Gramps loved to travel and my mother inherited the trait. I used to think I loved it too until my grandfather passed away. That's when I realized I just loved the stories. I loved listening to his stories on the way to make new ones.

In the middle of her telling me to spill the details

about Griffin's supposed girlfriend, I hit a pothole and my gaze shifts to the rearview as I watch the boxes shift under the rope that's got them all tied down in the bed of the truck.

Hissing in a curse rather than saying it in front of my mother, I keep my eye on the rearview for a moment longer. Everything in the back all steadies and I don't think anything shifted too much.

"You tied it all down, didn't you?"

I don't bother answering. It's not long until her mind drifts to Gramps as well.

"Your grandfather talked about the sailing competitions down here once."

"I know. It's one of the reasons we picked this place. Did he compete?"

"No … he wanted to, though. You know him," she says, her tone picking up and getting lighter, "he wanted to do everything under the sun. The only thing that kept him back was my mother."

"I think he would've liked it down here," I tell my mom but in my head all I can see is Magnolia. I know he would have loved her. She's soft and sweet, but it's her laugh and the way it shines in her eyes that roped me in. She's innocent in a way that's addictive.

"I'm sure he would have, but couldn't you have chosen somewhere closer?" my mother fusses and I can feel her stare on me.

I dare to counter, suggesting, "You could always move."

"I just might," she says like it's a threat, and a smirk lifts my lips. "What I really want to know is ... do you think this place could be your forever?"

"My forever?" I don't know why I repeat the last bit. I know exactly what she means even as she gabs on about planting roots and buying a home to invest in.

I don't think about a damn bit of what she's saying when I answer her. All I think about are Magnolia and Bridget.

"Yeah, Mom. I think this could be my forever."

CHAPTER
Ten

Magnolia

WHEN YOUR HEART'S A MESS, everything else in life is too. "One day you're going to fall in love. That boy better not break your heart."

Lying on the large sectional with Bridget, my statement isn't heard by a soul. I tuck the throw up to her chin and listen to her soft protest in her sleep as I sit up, leaving her there, snoozing away like she has so many times on Autumn's sofa.

The drone of a Disney movie can still be heard out here in the living room from her den, but Bridget is a good sleeper and I doubt she'll stir when I pick her up to take her home in a few hours.

A peek in the den reveals one kid still awake, wide eyed and obsessed, mouthing every line. All the others are asleep or nodding off.

"She's down for the count?" Sharon asks, her second glass of red in one hand while she offers me a glass of sangria with the other.

I gladly accept and nod before taking a small sip. "Yup."

I won't be fooled by Autumn's sangria. I once thought there'd be less alcohol in it than the wine. It was a night to remember and led to great memories, but a hangover from hell. One glass will do just fine tonight.

"Cheers to Wine Down Wednesday," Sharon says in a singsong voice, her glass clinking against mine.

"It's Friday."

"I don't care," Sharon responds in the same tone, her smile staying in place and forcing me to crack a wide smile as well.

"Firepit is going and the monitors are already set up." I follow her lead and head to the back patio, where the other women are circled around the just started firepit. The small flames have barely caught and Renee takes it upon herself to poke the hunks of wood, shifting them and working her magic.

My mind is busy wondering if Brody likes firepits when I catch Autumn checking the baby monitor.

Her little Cameron is only a few months old. I imagine the cup of coffee is for her, just so she can stay awake.

The breeze is just right, a small chill in the air that makes it the perfect throw blanket weather.

"Anyone need a refill?" Sharon questions and while the other women answer, I stare at the fire.

I had my first kiss by a firepit. Asher, way back in tenth grade, threw a party. His dad is real laid back. The kind of laid back where we all knew there would be older kids drinking and a cup or two would find its way over to us. If he happened to see, he'd make sure none of us were driving or getting so drunk we'd be sick. That was the extent of his monitoring. Looking back on it now, I wonder what the heck he was thinking letting teens drink in the airplane hangar, but truthfully, I'm pretty sure his dad started drinking at the same age he started working, which was right around fourteen according to him.

My father would have never allowed such a thing. Truth be told, I was scared to even take a sip from my red Solo cup. If he found out, he'd be livid. Robert was with me, though. We were all seated around the firepit. His hand landed on my knee, his thumb rubbing back and forth against my ripped jeans and I leaned into him. He was so warm, warmer than the fire even. My heart raced and when I kissed him it

107

was like everyone else had disappeared. I'll never forget that kiss.

Of course the second it was over, someone shouted that we were making out and my cheeks turned bright red. Robert threw something at him. I forget who it was but I remember laughing. I remember feeling loved.

"And then she said, 'You know the one good thing about being pregnant is that you get to avoid a lot of sex,' and my jaw just hung open." Autumn's statement snaps my attention back to the present.

"Oh my God, your aunt said that." Renee's expression of mortified shock is echoed on all our faces.

"RIP her sex life." Sharon somehow appears right on time with the perfect comment and a glass of red for Renee.

"I know!" Autumn's eyes are wide with emphasis while flipping back her cropped hair. She just got it cut and dyed blond last week. She may have just had a baby, but she's looking like a bombshell. The slouchy drape of her shirt certainly adds to that, even if she is only in burgundy flannel PJs.

The baby monitor lights up and steals the show before I can ask who they're talking about.

Tucking my left leg under my bottom, I get comfy on the wicker love seat. Renee has the other half of it, while Autumn and Sharon occupy two of the three seats that form a semicircle around the other side of the stone firepit.

"Who's the other chair for?" I ask Renee when Autumn shows Sharon the monitor with proof Cameron is sound asleep.

"Brianna just got home."

It takes me a second to realize Autumn's talking about her younger sister. Just as I'm about to comment I didn't know she was back from college, Autumn addresses her via the monitor. "Do you need me, Bri?"

I can barely hear her response, but whatever it is, Autumn doesn't move from her seat. From what I gather it was something to the effect of: take a chill pill and let me hold my nephew.

"So ..." Autumn lengthens and draws out the short, single word until I peek up at her from behind the rim of my glass midsip. She orders, "Update."

"About what?"

The group's collective sigh is far too extreme for the situation.

"You've got to have some goods to share."

Renee stays mum but I don't have to peek at her to know she's eating this up.

"Well, in short," I say then pause for effect, "I'm an absolute mess."

"So same old, same old," Sharon says, holding up her glass in cheers and I let out a good laugh.

"For real, though," I say then hesitate and lean over to a matching wicker basket full of throws to grab one to hide under. "I don't know what the hell I'm doing or how things got to be such a mess."

Sharon initiates the interrogation, asking, "So … which one are you dating?"

"I don't think she's actually dating them … are you dating them?" Autumn half answers for me, then backtracks.

"Well, let her answer and we'll know," Sharon mock scolds Autumn and then all eyes are on me.

I have not had *nearly* enough to drink to get into all this.

"You have been seeing Robert, right?" Sharon's eyes are narrowed like she's trying to remember. "Like recently? Or no?"

Renee knows everything, on a weekly, daily, and even sometimes hourly basis. But Autumn and Sharon have their shit together and a million things constantly going on. Occasionally they ask if I've seen Robert and sometimes I give them the details, and sometimes I just shrug. I suppose the main deciding factor is how much I've had to drink and how I'm feeling at that very moment.

"We've been off and on for a while."

"Right, but what about the sex?" Sharon isn't beating around the bush and judging by Autumn's expression, she's surprised she's being so blunt.

I'm not. She's a few cups deep, mellow and ready for gossip. To give it and to get it both. If one thing is true about her, Sharon is honest and shameless.

"Also off and on, but like … more on than off, up until Brody."

"'Cause you're having sex with Brody?" Sharon guesses and Autumn purses her lips before she smacks Sharon with a teal paisley outdoor pillow. It just barely misses Sharon's glass.

"Not the drink," Sharon jokes and raises it above her head. Renee lets out a small laugh.

"Let her tell you what she wants to tell you," Autumn mutters and then focuses on me when she adds, "You don't have to tell Miss Nosy a damn thing if you don't want to."

"I feel like I should, though," I confess as a bundle of nerves slowly tangles in the pit of my stomach. My fingers find the hem of the chenille throw blanket and I tell them, "I've slept with Brody. I've slept with Robert in the last month … and I don't know if I'm dating or if it's casual." My throat gets tight and a little dry, so I take a sip. The girls are quiet so there's only the crack and snap of the firepit to break up the tension. With a deep breath out, I add, "I think

I'm seeing both of them. Robert in a more serious way than before, because he's wanting more when he hasn't before. And Brody in a … I don't even know what way." I have to set my glass down on the side table in order to pull my hair back. "It's getting a little hot over here," I comment as I fan myself and Sharon laughs.

"I'll say. Look at you, girl." Sharon's pride is evident and her smile somehow broadens when I look back at her. "The best of both worlds," she says as if it's not a pickle I'm in. Like it could just go on forever like this. Oh my Lord, there is no way it can go on like this for much longer.

"For the longest time, you were the one not getting any. And now you're probably getting more than any of us."

"Speak for yourself," Autumn says and playfully smacks Sharon with the pillow once again, although this time it lacks force.

"Hot damn," Renee pipes up, aiding in changing the direction of the conversation. "So everyone's getting some."

"Wait, what?" I have to take in what she's said twice. "You and Griffin?"

"No." Renee's quick to backpedal, saying, "No, I mean you guys. I'm not with Griffin."

"What's going on there?" Sharon asks, leaning in and now the object of focus has become Renee.

"There's nothing there," Renee responds calmly, stealing some of my throw blanket for herself. "And we were talking about Magnolia."

Traitor! I can't help the bubble of laughter. "Throw me to the wolves, why don't ya?"

"Now we're wolves?" Autumn pulls both of her legs up to sit cross-legged in her seat. "Look what you did, Sharon. Now we're wolves." She chuckles into her glass and it's infectious.

"I'm sorry," Sharon says, holding up both hands. "I just want to know what's going on so I know who to root for is all." Her bare feet pad on the flagstone as she gets up to reach for her own throw. As the sun sets behind us even further, the solar lights switch on and in an instant, it feels that much cooler.

Renee takes her place at the fire again, poking and prodding the flames along.

"I don't even know who to root for," I tell them. "It's … it's just a mess and I don't know. Neither of them have said anything about dating or boy-friend-girlfriend shenanigans."

"Do people still use that phrase?" Autumn questions.

"Boyfriend and girlfriend?" Renee clarifies.

I can only shrug, and Sharon peeks up from over her glass to find us all waiting for an answer.

"What was the question?" she asks and Autumn leans her head back against the headrest then moans, "Oh my word, someone help this woman."

"In all seriousness, though, I think Mags is going through a lot and maybe that's why it's a bit different?"

"From the outside looking in, it seems like it," Autumn says, nodding in agreement.

I tell them, "It's just been a lot recently … because of Bridget."

Sharon nods and comments, "Well, that makes sense."

"Do you have the results yet?" Autumn asks at the same time that Sharon asks, "… So, this Brody. He's *the* Brody. For sure, for sure." That's already been established via text messages over the past week in bits and pieces. Girls' night was desperately needed.

"Not yet, and correct," I answer and then pick my glass back up, gathering my thoughts.

Autumn says, "So … Brody is like the new hot guy who's also an old flame?"

"But then there's Robert, and we all know that's never really been over," Sharon adds. Every bottle of wine that's ever graced this patio knows Robert's never really been out of the picture.

"Robert really asked you to marry him?" Autumn asks and I know she must be feeling the alcohol because we've all already covered this in text messages. So I just nod.

"I feel guilty just thinking about it."

"What did he say?" Sharon asks, seeming to sober up as she pulls her hair into a ponytail. "Like, he had to have said something to go from zero to one hundred."

"He brought up a promise he made years ago. He said we were meant to be together."

"He played with your heartstrings," Renee chimes in.

"That he did." I take a deep breath and then a long gulp of red.

Autumn, cross-legged and glass of wine in her hand, asks a question I've thought about since the moment I stood up from the table. "If Brody hadn't shown up, would you have said yes?"

All the girls lean in. It's so quiet all I can hear is the sizzle and snap of burning wood in the sputtering firepit while my heart runs away again. That's all it's done lately. It's trying to escape the torture I'm putting it through.

I don't have to think it through to know the answer to that question.

"Yeah," I answer and my throat feels dry all of a

sudden. Too dry for a single gulp of wine to quench it, so I take more sips of the sweet red. "If Robert had asked me any time in the past year, I could see saying yes to him, but wanting to keep it a secret for a bit. To ease into it publicly, you know?"

Autumn sighs and I bring my gaze to her, only to find her lips in a pout. "I'm sorry." Her attempt to console me isn't needed. I'm aware of how awful that truth is.

"Don't be. I don't think he would have proposed if it wasn't for Brody coming around." The truth is a hard pill to swallow, but it doesn't mean I can change it.

"Men are weird about marking their territory," Sharon comments and I think she means it to be funny. I have to admit it elicits a small laugh from me.

"That's one way to put it," I say.

Renee huffs a sarcastic laugh. "He could have started with asking you to be his girlfriend—"

"Does anyone do that anymore nowadays?" Sharon questions, interrupting Renee. "It seems more like … the olden days."

"The olden days?" Autumn's expression is one of horror.

Completely ignoring her, Sharon continues to lighten the mood. "Who's better in bed?" She points at me with the hand that's also holding her glass of wine. Or rather the glass that used to hold wine since it's empty now. With a straight face and a narrowed gaze she adds, "That one wins."

I can't help the smile that stretches across my heated face and I cover it with both hands, leaning into the outdoor throw pillow as I do. I clutch it to my chest when I slowly sit back upright.

My girlfriends are crazy and put me on the spot sometimes, but they have good hearts and even better senses of humor.

A few moments pass of easier conversation and the town's latest rumor regarding Autumn's sister Bri and Asher ... which is surprising to me, but the second it all settles down, Renee brings the issue back up.

"Do you have a plan?" Renee questions, bringing back an air of seriousness although I know she's only asking because she's my friend.

"I don't have a plan, which is why it feels so ..."

"Chaotic?"

"Yeah." I'm quick to agree with Sharon. It really does feel like chaos, and I'm not sure how it's going to end without me being wrecked beyond repair.

"Love is chaotic." She sways in her seat, a simper across her face at the statement that drives me crazy, yet spoken as if it's romantic.

Chaos isn't a good thing. Chaos is booming

thunderstorms and damaging winds. It's messy to the point of brokenness. Yes, that's what love is at first. And it's terrifying.

"Well maybe you don't need a plan," Sharon suggests.

Autumn agrees. "Yeah. Just see what happens."

"What do you think, Renee?" Sharon asks and I look to my lifelong friend who knows more of the sordid details than anyone else.

"I think … let's see what happens. Just do what feels right, because you are the one that has to live with it. Not either of those men. Not even little Bridget, and I know you don't like me bringing her up when it comes to things … that you might regret. But seriously. You need to look out for you because you're the one who's going to be in your head every night before bed wondering and worrying."

"Yeah." I whisper my response, lacking the confidence I know I should have at that suggestion.

Renee's expression is riddled with concern, but she softens it to add, "Does that make sense? I'm a little drunk."

"I've always tried to do what felt right. I can keep that up."

"There is no right or wrong when it comes to love." Sharon adds another romanticized line I'm not certain I agree with, even if she's staring off into the distance like the line is swoonworthy.

"Back to your sister," I say, turning the attention to Autumn and then nestle back down in my seat, letting Renee's advice really sink in. "Asher is never going to settle down, so I don't know why she's barking up that tree."

"Probably because it's a long, hard tree," Sharon says, emphasizing *long* and *hard* and instantly the tense situation evaporates.

It's then that Robert messages me.

Can I swing by? I want to tell you something.

My response is instant: *I'm at Autumn's.* The second I send it, though, I think about Brody and guilt worms its way in. They both know about each other. I don't know what to tell them, but I don't have the answers and it's too much pressure to feel like I should. Love is complicated and a tangled freaking mess.

The girls laugh as Sharon tells a story, and I pull my legs into my chest, letting out a laugh of my own although I'm not listening and I have no idea what she's saying.

Robert doesn't respond right away although he's seen the message, and all I can think is that I love him—for years I have loved him. If Brody wasn't in the picture, I absolutely would have said yes. I would have married him, and that weighs heavily on my mind.

It's nearly nine at night and I should get going, given that tomorrow is going to be a long day. I ask him, *You okay?*

He answers that question immediately: *Yeah, I'm all right, Mags. Just wanted to talk if you had the time.*

I want to talk too. I know I need to talk to him. There's so much that should have been said years ago and tears prick my eyes at the thought.

I text him and then prepare myself for a difficult conversation I wish I didn't have to have: *Let me get home and get Bridget in bed, come by in like half an hour?*

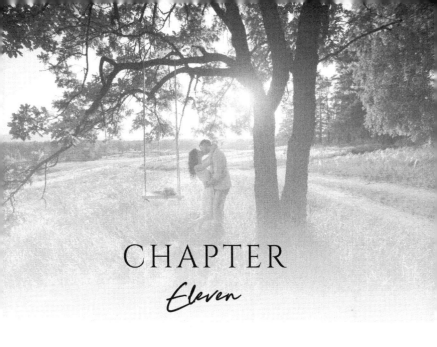

CHAPTER
Eleven

Magnolia

I DON'T KNOW EXACTLY WHERE TO START, BUT Robert needs to know that I don't know where I stand. I love him, I've always loved him, but I don't know if it's enough. The worst part is that I feel awful for not knowing. It's a pain I don't think I've ever felt.

He deserves better. There are plenty of ways I could start the conversation. They run wild in the back of my mind as I dip a bag of tea into steaming water and then stare at the clock on the stove.

My nightshirt is my most conservative one. I would have stayed in my clothes if they didn't smell like smoke. With no makeup on, my skin still pink from freshly scrubbing it, and my baby girl in bed, I'm ready for bed more than anything. My eyes are so heavy, I could sleep a million years. Yet the anxiousness would keep me wide awake. I think until I get these thoughts out of me, it'll keep me up.

Sometimes the truth just needs to be spoken. It feels like a breakup, not because I want it to end, but because this situation no longer serves either of us. I realize that as I make my way to the sofa and pull the thin chenille throw over myself, steaming teacup in hand. I love him, but I think I'm in love with someone else as well. There's no way anyone would ever be okay with that.

At that thought, the front door opens slowly and quietly. I told him to come on in. I'm halfway up off the couch when our eyes meet. I'm sure mine express the doubt and insecurities that have burrowed themselves in every thought.

I wasn't prepared for the sight of him.

He motions for me to sit back down, quietly closing the door. With one hand running through his hair and the other tossing keys onto the foyer table, the strong man I've always known is nothing but as he swallows thickly, the cords in his neck tightening.

His eyes are rimmed with red when they meet mine again for only a split second. He glances down the hall as he slips off his windbreaker, leaving him in dark taupe khakis and a pale blue polo that matches his eyes.

"You okay?" I can't help the concern that overwhelms me seeing him like that. My immediate thought is that something happened with his mother. He doesn't like to talk about it, and I didn't consider it with everything else going on. He's come over more than a half dozen times this late, simply not to be alone after spending the day with her.

"Yeah, is she asleep?" he asks softly, sitting down opposite me in the armchair. I'm grateful for the distance.

"She's passed out," I answer him and search his eyes for what's wrong. Is it us? Is it something worse? "What's going on?"

A sad smile graces his lips as he leans back. "That's a loaded question, isn't it?" Resting his head on the back of the chair, he avoids my gaze and stares at the ceiling instead.

"I'm sorry," he says before anything else and I'll be damned if I don't feel selfish at the sight of him falling apart. "I didn't want to come," he starts as I set the teacup down and scoot to the edge of the sofa closest to him and with my bottom barely on the cushion at all. Slipping my hand to his knee, I tell him it's okay.

"Mom's not doing well and I know you have enough on your plate right now, but—"

"You can always come here." I say what I've told him for years, but a pang of regret hits me hard in my chest. The same thought must hit him as well, because he finally looks at me and admits, "I'm not so sure that I should, though."

I start to protest, but his strong hand lands on mine and he says, "It's all right, Mags."

"Robert—"

"I get it." He cuts me off again, his thumb running soothing circles on my knuckles. "I can't seem to do the right thing." At that statement, he pulls his hand away and both of them cover his face. "I knew I shouldn't come because it's already too much, but I couldn't stay away."

He swallows thickly, holding back emotion that's already shining in his glossy eyes. "I know it's selfish, but I just needed—" his last word is choked and he throws his head back, covering his face again and cursing.

"It's okay—"

"It's not, though. You asked me for time and I'm afraid if I give it to you, I'll lose you forever."

His confession knocks me completely off-balance and I pull my hand back only a fraction, but he's quick to grab it, holding on to it. Our eyes meet, the pain between us palpable, each of us afraid of losing the other.

It's quiet, too quiet as all pretenses leave us and I usher out the confession I know is going to tear us apart. "I love you, but I think I love him too."

Never in a million years would I have thought he'd respond the way he does. "I know." He licks his bottom lip, taking in a slow, steadying breath. "I know, and that's why I shouldn't have come, but I love you."

Tears slip out from the corners of my eyes and I have to pull my hand away to wipe them as I attempt to gather myself and calm my racing thoughts.

My chest rises and falls with staggered breaths and I reach for my tea, focusing on it rather than Robert's apology when he says, "I wanted to tell you I'm sorry. I'm sorry I didn't fight harder. I'm sorry I ... I'm sorry I wasn't better, Mags. If I could go back," he starts and I murmur his name in a plea for him to stop. He does.

"I'm sorry too," I manage to get out and without taking a sip of the now warm tea, I set it back down, sniffling and steadying myself. I am grateful for honesty, even if it doesn't help a darn thing. I can feel him slipping away, the distance between us growing even though neither of us dares to move.

"I shouldn't have come over, but I couldn't just let him—" Robert stops himself from finishing whatever he was going to say.

"Him. Him as in Brody?" I ask to clarify and I'm almost certain I know what he was going to say.

Brody changes everything, and it feels like my heart's breaking all over again.

"I've been trying to do the right thing. It's just ... I can't not love you, Mags. I tried. As fucked up as it sounds, I tried to not love you when you told me you didn't want me. When you—" He stops abruptly, not completing his thought. Slowly, his pale blue eyes meet mine and he admits to me, "I tried to not love you once and it killed me. I can't do it, Mags. Even if you love him too, I can't help loving you."

Robert's never been a man of emotion. He is logic and reason. He is comfort without needing to say a word. Yet here he is, laying bare things I wish he would have said so long ago.

"What can I do?" He's always helped me. Even when I hated myself and when I didn't have anything at all to give him in return, he came through. There's not a lot of people in the world who can say they have someone like that. To see him like this utterly shreds me. "What can I do so that you don't stop loving me?"

"I don't think I could ever not have love for you," I speak slowly. The way I said *have love*, seems to strike him.

"I'm sorry about … the other night."

Before I can tell him it's all right and that I'm sorry too, before I can explain how it caught me off guard, he heaves in a deep breath, noticeably distressed and adds, "I don't want you to hate me again. I need you."

"I've never hated you," I speak over him, reaching out to him to stress that point as I shake my head in complete disagreement.

Robert doesn't look me in the eyes although his strong hands wrap around mine, covering them with a warmth that's absent between us.

I hate it all. I hate the way this feels and I just want it to stop. I used to think when you love someone, seeing them in pain is the worst thing in the world. But it's not. When you love someone, the worst thing is when you're aware that you're the one putting them in pain. It's an awful feeling, so awful I imagine it's what death feels like. "Why does this feel like goodbye?" I manage to speak and I wish I hadn't said it out loud, but I suppose we're being honest tonight.

"I don't want to say goodbye. I don't want there to be anything ..." his voice hitches slightly before he pauses and I can tell he's holding back.

"I'm not saying goodbye ... you're my—" I almost say "best friend," but I stop myself short. It's more than that, or different.

"I'm just sorry and I wish we could go back. You know that I love you, don't you?"

There are different kinds of love. I know that all too well. The way I love him and the way I love Renee compared to the way I love Bridget ... it's all different, but it's still love.

"I do, and I love you, Robert. I love you so much—" In an instant he leans forward, his arms pulling me close as he slips off the chair and lands on his knees in front

127

of me. His fingers grip the curves of my waist, his touch hot and desperate, yet somehow steadying me. He rests his forehead against mine with his eyes closed, and I'm trapped in this moment.

There's a moment of time before he kisses me, a moment where I know I could stop him, a moment where I know he's waiting for approval … it's the moment I lean forward, closing my own eyes and welcoming the familiar comfort to ease our pain. My lips mold against his and when he sweeps his tongue across the seam of my lips, I part them, granting him entry. Shifting forward, he pulls me in closer and my hands land against his strong shoulders to keep me steady. It's something I'm used to, yet somehow it feels new and unexpected. His touch is tender as his hands splay against my back and the swell of my breasts press against his hard chest.

He deepens the kiss, his tongue sweeping against mine in passionate stokes. The groan that escapes him is full of hunger and instantly my nipples pebble, my core heats and I want him. I'd be a liar if I said otherwise. Heat consumes me instantly, so I pull back, needing to breathe in cooler air. Leaving an openmouthed kiss on my neck, he drags his teeth down my skin and it brings me to the edge of need.

His hands drop down to my thighs, his fingers running along the hem before he pulls back and I lower my gaze to his. The first boy I loved and gave myself to, the man who's held me up when I couldn't stand, and the lover I've kept for years looks back at me longingly.

"I love you, Magnolia," he whispers.

Reality slips its way in, only a fraction, but it's enough to push the words out, words that he needs to know.

"I slept with him." Swallowing thickly, I tell him again, "I slept with Brody."

A moment passes and I'm not certain Robert's heard me. "He wants to see me tomorrow … after the gala at the after-party."

The cords in his neck tighten as he swallows. It's his only reaction as my heart races, slamming in protest with each harsh beat.

"That's okay," he finally responds just above a murmur. "It's complicated, but," he licks his lower lip, his tone calm and accepting, "that's okay," he repeats. I don't expect him to kiss me again, let alone to whisper at the shell of my ear, "Sleep with him, do whatever you want with him. But tell me if he does something you like. I'll do it better and when I'm done with you, you'll forget all about him."

The chill of the air caresses my neck in the absence of his heat as he pulls away. One beat and then another passes with his gaze focused on me, trapping me and tempting me. The intensity is all too much.

"I don't want to go anywhere without you, Mags."

His baby blues drop to my lips before meeting my eyes again and he adds, "I don't want to lose you."

There's a spark inside of me that's always been his. It'll never die and it rages with need and understanding when he leans forward for another kiss. Robert pauses, brushing the tip of his nose against mine. "Please, let me love you."

With memories and promises, with everything we've been through clouding my judgment as much as lust is, I lean forward, silencing him and crush my lips against his.

His fingertips are careful and gentle as they brush against my thighs, slipping the thin fabric of my night-shirt up higher.

I inhale a deep breath, my head falling back, and submit to what feels right in this moment. Even if it also feels wrong.

His lips trail down my neck as my nails scratch down his back, wanting his shirt off, needing to feel his skin against mine. My body knows his and as he lays me down on the sofa, everything feels right and need takes over. It's a desperate need to know how we feel together that fuels the fire.

My neck arches and for a moment, I have a glimpse at what happens next. What happens after this mo-ment is only a memory, and my heart shatters. My lips desperately seek his to keep the thought at bay, but for a moment I felt the pain strike me in an instant.

My heart breaks in a way where I know it's saying goodbye. That he came here to say goodbye in a way and instead I held on. If only I don't move, if only we stayed here forever, the shards of my heart wouldn't fall, they'd stay right where they should. But we can't stay here like this. There's so much more to life than the whispered declarations of two kids in love making promises they can't keep.

"I love you," he reminds me in between heated kisses and that's all I need to cling to him and get lost in the moment again. Simply loving him back like I have all my life is all I need to think about for tonight.

CHAPTER
Twelve

Magnolia

"ALL IS FAIR IN LOVE AND WAR" IS A downright dirty lie.

I know darn well what happened last night wasn't fair.

There's nothing fair about having your heart ripped out of your chest, and I feel every bit of that pain as I stand here.

The lights are dim enough to feel romantic, yet the spotlights showcase each piece with pride. The music is soft enough for the chatter to carry throughout the space, yet the bass is felt just slightly.

The aroma of sweet wine and delicate hors d'oeuvres expertly passed around on silver trays is subtle, yet appetizing. Everything for the gala is perfect. It's as if I've plucked it from my dreams and delivered it on one of those silver platters myself.

And yet all I can focus on in this moment is the fact that Brody is waiting for me back at his bar once I close down the event.

It feels like I've betrayed him. Even if I was with Robert first. Even if he knows I care for Robert and he cares for me in return. Even if we aren't exclusive. All is not fair in love. Maybe there's nothing fair about love at all.

Still, I did what my heart wanted me to and it felt right, even if it felt like goodbye.

"Literally gorgeous," Mandy repeats for at least the fourth time tonight, her flattened hand gesturing twice in the packed space with the tips of her fingers pointed up to the ceiling. She's three champagne glasses in and it's noticeable, given that the fluttering hand nearly smacks against her husband's glass. He's quick to avoid the disaster and he gives her a smirk, his arm wrapped around her waist. Sean pulls her in tighter as she continues.

"I knew putting my faith in you was the right thing to do." Her comment comes with a vigorous nod.

I'm not going to lie, I'm grateful she went out ahead of time with Samantha and a few other artists. From what I've gathered through social media, Sam's a heavy drinker and it appears that my boss tried to keep up with her. It also appears her husband finds it humorous as he tucks his tie back inside of his jacket, just in time for her to tug it out again playfully. Her hands haven't left him since they walked in. All in all, that means the pressure I felt before she walked in has greatly subsided.

"Is there anything you need me to do?" Mandy questions, straightening and seemingly sober for a moment, as if she just heard my thoughts.

With a quick shake, I widen the smile I've had plastered on my face for the last hour and answer, "Not a thing."

Which is true. I've hired help for the night. A great deal of the budget actually went to labor costs. It started with a whirlwind of men helping me set up three hours ago, and it'll end with a cleaning crew in the morning. Only three pieces have yet to sell of over twenty on display; the night has just begun as most guests didn't arrive until just a half hour ago.

"Everything's going perfectly," I say and the response to Mandy feels like a lie, but not because of the event. Literally every aspect is just how I wanted it to be. It's perfect, but I'm not faring as well.

It's the fact that Robert walked in five minutes ago, brushing elbows with a couple. The man is in a tailored dark gray suit that's obviously expensive, but pales in comparison to the dress perfectly hugging his companion's curves. It's seductive and a bit overdressed for a cocktail event, but gorgeous nonetheless. It's better to be overdressed than under, anyway. I imagine he's the politician in for the weekend whom Robert's planned to woo.

The second I laid eyes on him, he smiled at me, this charming and confident smile. It breaks my heart because I don't want to take that smile away from him, but after last night, I know things have to change between us. Even if he doesn't want it to.

"Enjoy the night, dear." My boss barely gets out the words with a quick squeeze of my shoulder before calling out "There you are," and brushing past, her husband in tow, to greet someone behind me. She's a mess, but a delighted mess so I'll take it.

"Don't worry, I've got her," her husband, Sean, assures me with an equally delighted smile and a hint of his Southern accent. He's tall with dark hair and watching them together ... they pair perfectly.

I failed to tell her about the surprise, but how can I possibly think straight knowing Robert is right there? My cowardly heart wishes things were different. I wish I'd known how this was going to end years ago. Hindsight really is twenty-twenty.

"You didn't sleep a wink." I jump at Renee's voice, my hand flying to my chest. She's right, I didn't sleep at all after Robert left. The reality of it all made me play out how the scene will go tonight when I confess it all to Brody.

With my lips parted, I swear I planned on making a joke about sleep, but not a word comes out and Renee's eyes go big.

"You had sex with Brody," she guesses in a hushed whisper, glee clear on her face.

With my lips pressed in a thin line, I shake my head gently and that glee vanishes, her brow climbing as high as it can go.

"Oh. Em. Gee. With Robert?" The shock on her face is exacerbated by her jaw remaining dropped. Her cherry-red lips match the fifties-style pinup dress.

"How the heck can you even tell I had sex," I mutter in disbelief as she snags a second glass of champagne, throwing it back at my admission by lack of denial.

Blinking several times, she practically hisses her whisper with a scrunched-up expression, "You slept with Robert?"

"I ..."

"The gala is going well." Sharon's voice is heard at the same time her hip bumps against mine, breaking into our invisible confessional booth.

The pop of a champagne bottle accompanied by a round of applause steals my attention. The man of conversation is responsible for the interruption. Robert's found the bottle I stowed away for him behind the bar to impress whomever it is he's attempting to persuade. Judging by the glimpse of pearly whites and nods, I think it's going well for him.

I hope it is.

"You should become an event planner." Sharon speaks up again before taking a sip of the bubbly. Her sleek red dress matches Renee's lips, but Sharon opted for a nude shade on hers. It's nearly eight now and the first thought I have, glancing at the clock on my phone, is that Brody's bar is opening up now for the first time. Why last night of all the nights? Questions, regrets and unknowns swarm my head every empty second as the clock ticks on.

Sharon's gaze finally lands on Renee's expression and she rights herself to ask, "What did I miss?"

"Ladies," Robert's voice greets us just in time for the crowd to gather, Renee to my left and Sharon to my right. "I promised the director of administrations I'd introduce him to the planner of tonight's event." His crisp navy suit is my favorite of all the ones he owns because it frames his shoulders perfectly, and he's wearing the dark gray tie I got him last Christmas. He slips his hand down it before smoothing his jacket as he introduces each of us, including Renee and Sharon.

Everything about him is easygoing and the group around him is relaxed. He has a way of doing that. He's always been charming, polite and handsome. A tingle travels down my neck and across my shoulders just hearing his voice. The words that kept me up at night lay at the tip of my tongue, begging to be spoken. Swallowing them down, I manage a warm, "Thank you for coming."

"My dear, this event is lovely," Marc comments and I note that he's much older than Robert, the wrinkles around his eyes giving proof to years of experience. Even still, he possesses the same charm and charisma.

Sharon's a bit tipsy and pulls an adorable curtsy that's rewarded with a chuckle from the far too sober director, but a great warmth from the woman on his arm. The woman Robert introduced as Olivia tells me, "I love everything about tonight." She speaks with an accent I can't place. Her makeup is subdued and natural compared to her attire, but not a strand is out of place in her simple but chic bun.

"Thank you, and I love your accent," I tell her and the compliment only makes her smile broader. Perfect pearly whites shine back.

"Thank you. My husband stole me away from Spain years ago." She gazes lovingly at Marc and I wonder what their love story is. I wonder if mine would resonate with her. Leaving the thoughts in my head where they belong, I listen to Robert boast about the art programs in town and the changes they've made to some bill that's up for debate.

Wining and dining come naturally to him, and he converses with the couple and the two other gentlemen easily. Renee has disappeared but Sharon's enthralled with Olivia, and the two of them seem to hit it off right from the start.

It's when Olivia raises her glass in cheers that I spot the ring. It's quite a large diamond that sparkles in the light as the glasses clink. Again, I find myself absorbed by thoughts of marriage like I never have before. Thoughts of Brody in front of me, teasing me, flicker in my mind. Although, if I were him, I don't know how I'd react to last night.

"Robert tells me you're an expert in this," Marc says, interrupting my thoughts, and gestures around the room. "The … art my wife goes on about," he adds and his statement comes out sounding like a question.

I blink twice, wondering if he means all art.

"She's aggressive in her desire to save the arts," he elaborates with a tone that tells me he's not certain he agrees.

"Oh, I see," I say and nod, noting he still hasn't touched his drink and he's certainly here for more business … at least for the moment. "Well, I have to agree with her, and she's certainly a woman with good taste."

"That she is." The endorsement brings back his smile and the glass finally makes its way to his lips. His gaze settles on his wife's backside. The moment that glass comes down, though … I wish he'd downed it and taken Olivia to the inn like he obviously wants to do.

"So, you two?" he questions, the glass in his hand motioning between Robert and me.

"Marc." Robert's tone is one meant to put a halt to that questioning and steer the conversation elsewhere.

"What?" He draws back slightly, clearly defending his statement. "I see the way you look at her."

My heart does that pitter-patter and I steal a glass of champagne to hide behind from a tray passing by. My first of the night. I promised myself I wouldn't touch an ounce of alcohol during the event, but my nerves are shot.

"We're good friends." Robert's response feels two-fold. Both a shield to protect me, and yet it's a knife to my heart all the same. Hasn't it always felt like that, though?

The director's eyebrows raise and he shakes his head as if he doesn't believe him. "If that's the way you want it then."

"Excuse me," I say and I'm as polite as I can manage. Not that it matters; Robert knows me all too well. As I turn with an amiable nod to the two of them, Marc acknowledges my departure with a raise of his glass before turning his attention to his wife, but Robert follows me.

I wish I could outrun him and more importantly,

outrun the turmoil of hypocrisy that churns inside of me.

We're only friends. That's all we've ever told anyone for years. Only friends. What's changed is that I know for certain, that's all we were meant to be.

Last night we weren't, but what right do I have to a title more than friends, when I've told him that's all I want and I'm actively pursuing someone else? Someone who is more than likely going to be hurt by what I did last night, with my so-called friend.

"Mags," he says and Robert's hushed voice is laced with urgency.

The smile stays in place, although it's tight and it doesn't keep my eyes from pricking with tears that shouldn't be there. *Suck it up. Chin up. Push those feelings back down.*

"Yes?" I manage although my throat is dry and my heart hammers.

"Should I have said something else?" Robert asks me and I don't have an answer.

Yes, a voice from a younger me pleads. My head shakes, attempting to silence the decade-long thoughts.

"Tell me what I should do," he commands me although his tone is pleading. "Mags, please," he says, ignoring a patron who's brushed beside him and the clatter of glasses bumping against one another on a tray being carried off in the distance.

Not a word leaves me, because I don't have any. Life doesn't prepare you for moments like this. I'm barely surviving all by myself.

I can't manage to utter a darn word. Not a single one.

Robert's soft blue eyes meet mine, searching for something and in that moment, the crowd doesn't exist. There's no music, there's not a soul to distract us. I hope he can feel what I feel. It's torture, is what it is. That's what this kind of love is, it's torture.

CHAPTER
Thirteen

Brody

GRIFFIN'S NERVOUS TAPPING IS GRATING ON my last nerve. His thumb is making a constant *tap, tap, tap* on the side of his plastic cup. It's a custom plastic Solo cup. The date of our opening is boasted in thick black font on the signature red cups. If I had to name one thing I've learned about Griffin in the last month, it's that he's damn good with marketing.

Tonight has three purposes:

1. To give this town a taste of our draft beers, sold exclusively here.
2. Drive home the date we're opening.

3. Kiss Magnolia and make damn sure she knows
    how much I want her.

If driving up to Pennsylvania and back taught me anything, it's that I missed her. "We should've gone to the art thing," Griffin comments as another car door opens and a chick with a wide-brimmed sun hat climbs out, although the sun has long set.

My side-eye is strong at that remark. The bar is packed. Inside and out.

"Renee will be here," I reply and then stare at the empty cup in his hand. There's no doubt in my mind this place will be littered with them tomorrow when everyone leaves. Not that I give a shit about anything at this very moment other than Magnolia getting here. I'll worry about cleaning up when the time comes tomorrow.

"They're right down the street, we should have swung by."

I remind him, "We did."

"Peeking in the window so you could check in on her does not count." He adds, "Chicken," complete with a deadpan look.

Clearing my throat, I remind him that she told me it was fine not to come and that she'd be busy. I got back into town early this morning and slept most of the day away, so everything here was behind schedule. Still …

he's right, we could have dropped in for at least a look around, but the damn place was crowded.

"She'll be here," I repeat.

"The gala ended close to an hour ago," is Griffin's rebuttal.

"They said they'd be here," I tell him to soothe his nerves, but I might as well be talking to a mirror. I'd be lying if I didn't admit that I'm nervous to see them too. I thought for a half second earlier Magnolia would walk in while my mother was here, checking out the place. My own nerves were shot to hell at the thought of them bumping into each other. Obviously I knew that wasn't possible, since I was stuck here setting up and she was handling her business down the way.

There's a popular alternative station booming from the newly installed speakers, the ever-thickening crowd is chatting while drinking and we've got a bonfire in the back that most of the town seems to be drawn to. I'm surprised it all got approved so easily. Even the bonfire, which Griffin was worried about because of some law down here about open burning and recreational fires. With every mention of a paper that needed to be filled out, all I could hear was Robert's threat about how he's taking Magnolia away from me. Even if she says otherwise. The more I think about those two, the more Magnolia's resistance to me makes sense.

She loves him.

The unsettling feeling at that thought forces me to adopt Griffin's bad habit.

Tap, tap, tap. Our fingers don't quit fidgeting. Even as an older gentleman tips his hat to us before starting a conversation about the menu of the bar and how we should use local vendors, my thumb carries on in time with the beat of the music.

"I couldn't agree more," Griffin says, maintaining the conversation well enough without me doing much of anything but nodding along.

My gaze is focused past the man's jean jacket to the sidewalk where crowds come and go. The weather's perfect, the atmosphere is just right, the beer's damn good, and the town's filtering in, making itself right at home for a night out in our bar.

But one thing, one woman, is missing.

As if on cue, her sweet voice comes from behind me and breaks up the conversation. "There you are." Turning on my heel, I catch sight of Magnolia.

She must've come in through the back.

The cream silk top flows loosely down her front until it meets a high-waisted, pleated navy skirt. Her smile is shy as she tucks a strand of her hair, loose from the updo she's got it in, behind her ear. The perfect accessory isn't those fuck me heels she's wearing, it's the blush that creeps up her cheeks when she sees me. It

does something to me, something soothing, yet enthrall-
ing at the same time.

She may have loved Robert once but, at the very
least, she wants me right now.

"There you are," I say, giving her those words right
back to her and she brightens, her simper blooming
into a full-blown grin.

She's like sunshine. I remember thinking that years
ago, when I was waiting at the bar but she never came.
It was like I had a taste of sunshine for a single night.
Since then it's been only gray skies until recently.

"I've been looking for you," she says and her statement is tinged with a shy nervousness. Even her smile
that I love so much wavers. I don't like the feeling it
gives me.

Before I can even say hello to Renee beside her,
Griffin's already directing her to the bar. He didn't waste
any time at all. Judging by her smirk, Renee doesn't
mind in the slightest.

Although she glances at Magnolia, who nods
slightly, as if it's a covert signal, before allowing Griffin
to lead the way away from us.

Again, that nagging feeling that something's off
comes back.

"Everything go as planned tonight?"

"Yeah," she answers while glancing down at her

hands. Her fingers wring around one another. It reminds me of how she was that night four years ago.

Some things are the same about her, while others are different … and I've fallen for both versions.

"We swung by earlier," I admit to her and her blue eyes widen like she's sorry she didn't see us when she asks, "You did?"

"We didn't go inside to say hello. Griffin wanted—"

She waves off my apology before I can even finish. "Don't be," she says, breathing out and a soft blush rises to her cheeks. It's accompanied by a nervous huff and a seemingly forced smile.

"You all right?" I ask her, feeling the slight chill of the night. With the front doors wide open, the breeze blows in easily enough. Most of the crowd has filtered to the back, where the bonfire is raging and the makeshift dance floor is packed.

It's then I notice the goosebumps on Magnolia's arms. I wish I had a jacket to offer her. Thinking of the setup I have in the back, maybe I've got something better.

"I have to tell you something." Magnolia's ever-sweet simper fades and as her lips part, I stop her.

"Let's go to my office so I can hear you."

Biting down on her lower lip, she nods as I wrap my arm around her waist. It feels right there, and as she walks close to me, I savor the feel of her warmth.

"That's something I never thought I'd say," I add in an attempt to ease whatever is bothering her.

"What?"

"My office," I clarify.

A genuine smile lights up her face, but it only lasts a moment as I lead her through the crowd to the back. If she cares about anyone seeing us, she doesn't let it show. As I take a second look at her, I note that she doesn't seem to see them at all. Whatever she's thinking about has my girl in her own little world.

When I shut the door with a soft click, the music still filters through but it's quieter back here and warmer. The cameras are all set up so I can see if anyone comes down the slim hall to get back here.

I lock the door to make sure no one interrupts her and then I think maybe I should ask her if she minds, but she's busy admiring the barely furnished office.

The walls are devoid of decoration and it still smells like fresh paint. The closet door opens with a creak and I pull out a blanket, laying it down on the floor.

Besides the expensive-ass desk, there are only two cheap foldout steel chairs in the corner of the room. When I reach for the two glasses, my heart races. It's not much. Just a cozy blanket and champagne. I thought maybe no one from the town would bother to show and we could head out back, enjoy the fire together. It's insanity that the idea of no one coming didn't matter when I came up with this plan.

"I love the floors," Magnolia says and then turns, finally seeing the blanket as I pop open the bottle. "I don't think I told you." Her last words escape one by one, each one slower than the last.

Her fingers play with the ends of her hair. I've noticed it's a nervous habit of hers.

"A glass to celebrate," I say and lick my lower lip, pausing to remember how I was going to say it. Celebrate her success, my success ... But more so to celebrate us. The way shock stays on her expression and the happiness I thought would light her eyes is absent keeps those words from coming.

"Thanks," she replies and a nervous prick tickles the back of my throat. I clear it before pouring us each a glass. It fizzes just right.

"I'm always open to decorating advice if you have any," I offer, feeling my heartbeat pick up. That same nervousness that I'm going to lose her before we even get started clings to me as I offer her my hand to sit and then take my place beside her.

Tucking her skirt under her, she backs up to lean against the wall.

"Is this all right?" I ask her and she only nods. Both of her hands are wrapped around that glass like she's holding on to it for dear life.

There's something off. I know it. A crease settles in her brow before she says again that she has something to tell me, not taking a sip of the champagne.

I swear I can hear her heart pounding even though I'm a good two feet away from her. My first thought is that it has to do with the paternity test, but I would get those results same as she would and my phone hasn't gone off to notify me that I got an email.

She makes me nervous. No woman has ever gotten to me the way Magnolia does.

I blurt out, "Why does it feel like you're breaking up with me?"

"You didn't say I was your girlfriend," she says nearly defensively, but not quite. It's more with a knowing sadness and I hate it. Is that what's bothering her?

"You want me to put a label on it?" I nearly offer up the second option, "Or do you want to wait until the results come in?", but I swallow the words down. Damn do they taste bitter.

"Do you?" she asks back, but then shakes her head, gripping the edge of her chair and a seriousness playing on her expression. "I have to tell you something first."

"What's that?" The second I ask, a somber air takes over and I can't fucking stand being so far away from her. She parts her lips, heaving in a deep breath, but I stop her. "Hold that thought."

I scoot closer to her, setting my glass on the floor

and leaving it there. Then I lean forward and when I'm close enough, I brush my lips against hers in a peck of a kiss.

I know I have her when she tilts up her head, accepting it and then deepening it. When I pull back, her eyes are still closed, like she's still living in that moment.

She doesn't dare open them, even when she whispers something that tears at my insides. "I'm scared you aren't going to want me."

"Of course I want you."

"Not when—"

She starts to say something but I cut her off, hating the way her insecurity makes me feel. "What does your heart want?" I know what mine wants. I want her. Exactly how she is. I don't give a damn if it's not perfect like love is in the movies. Or if she had something going on with Robert and he thinks he has some claim to her. I don't give a fuck about anything else.

"To be happy and to make sure my little girl is happy and loved."

"If I'm her dad, I'll be here for her to make sure she's happy." *If I'm her dad …* The second statement of the night I never thought I'd utter.

"And if you're not?" she asks softly, her eyes finally opening. She swallows thickly and before she can repeat herself, I answer honestly. It's something that's kept me up at night, thinking that maybe I'm wrong, and Bridget isn't mine.

"I'll be here." I strengthen my voice and add, "I'm not leaving."

"Let me—" she stops and starts to put her glass down, like it overwhelms her that I admitted I want to be there regardless. Hell, her insecurity is contagious. It creeps up on me. "I have to tell you something and you're probably going to hate me for it."

It's not just that she frowns or that her voice hitches with anxiousness. It's the look in her eyes. There's fear and sadness and she's looking at me like that's what she expects from me. As if I'd ever want anything other than to see her smile.

"There's nothing you could say—"

"I slept with Robert."

Magnolia

"I slept with him … last night." The confession burns its way through me and there's not an ounce of relief once it's spoken. I feel like I could both cry and die at the same time.

No man has ever owned my emotions like he does.

There's an intense fear of disappointing him or hurting him, a fear of losing him that I can't escape.

Brody's silent at first, taking a moment to absorb what I just said. All the while I shrink down in size. Not because I'm ashamed of sleeping with two men, but because I'm worried that doing so hurt him.

I didn't mean for any of this to happen. It's been one reckless moment after another. "I'm sorry."

The small office feels hot in an instant. I keep reminding myself that I made my bed and I'm happy to lie in it, but without Brody giving me any kind of signal about how he feels, I'm dying inside.

"Can I be honest?" Brody asks and every red alert goes off as the anxious heat rises, and I prepare myself for whatever he has in store for me.

"Of course."

There's no judgment in his tone, only sincerity when he says, "I know you and him have something going on and—"

Cutting Brody off, I explain, "We have for years." All the memories bombard me. My exhale is shaky and I run my hands through my hair. "I didn't mean to last night, and I know since you've ... been here ... I've felt torn."

"Torn." He repeats that word, his gaze penetrating mine, holding me hostage.

"Yes," I answer softly.

"Because you love him?" he questions and I can only nod. "But you also … feel something for me too?" he asks and there's a hopeful spark in his eyes. It threatens to give me relief.

Again, I nod and whisper my answer.

"What are you and Robert?" he asks carefully and then reaches for his champagne. I didn't give him a moment to toast in celebration. His gaze drops for a moment, but rises with more hunger and seriousness than it had before. His fingers play at the rim of the champagne glass.

"We've always been good friends," I start, then pause to take in a deep, steadying breath.

"Could that be all you two will be?"

"Just friends?" I clarify and as he nods, he swallows, the cords of his neck tightening. There's a heated tension between us as I pick up my champagne glass too and take a sip before answering honestly, "Yes."

"What happened last night?"

"It's complicated." I wish I could tell him everything, but no one in this town knows what Robert's mother is going through. "It's not all my story to tell," I add.

"You could let me in, you know?"

"I want to," I admit to him and a wave of longing meets something else inside of me. This deep-seated fear that I'm already in too deep with Brody. It's hot and burns me from the inside out. I'm ready to give my love, all of it, to one man and the truth is, I trust Brody to take my heart fully, but once I give it to him, I don't know what will become of it if he were ever to give it back.

"So you slept with him?" Brody asks like it's a casual conversation and not our hearts on the line.

My throat's tight as I nod.

"And he knows … he knows we …?" He leaves the bit about the two of us being intimate unspoken.

"He does, yes." I'm quick to apologize. "I'm sorry. I didn't mean to hurt you. It wasn't about us and—"

"I want to call you Rose so bad right now," he says, cutting me off and then huffs a small laugh, repositioning on the blanket next to me so he's closer and leans against the wall.

"Rose?"

"Because there's so much about you that's the same since that night I met you." His nostalgic comment is warm and calms me slightly. "We weren't in a committed, monogamous relationship. I didn't put a label on it, as you pointed out."

"You don't hate me?"

"I could never hate you. And it's easy to see you have feelings for him, since you two have history … but he knows I want you, and you know I want you. I don't give a damn who you've been with before tonight, but I want you all to myself." A vulnerability shines in his doe eyes. "Are you good with that? That you're my girl-friend. And mine alone."

I nearly tell him I love him. I catch the words on their way up my throat and nearly choke on them. My smile hides behind the champagne glass as I take a gulp, but he must see it because he smiles broadly at the sight of me.

"I take it that's a yes?" he says, toying with me.

"Yes. I'd like to be your girlfriend," I answer him and my shoulders relax, my heart seems to dance in my chest and everything feels lighter at the thought. It feels right.

"How many men have you been with?" he asks me and I know I must turn fire-engine red given the heat that floods my cheeks.

"Two." I don't expect the shock that widens his eyes. "I'm a bit sheltered."

"A bit?" he jokes and I have to laugh at his ex-pression before leaning into him. He takes a sip of champagne and then wraps his arm around my waist, bringing me in closer to him. He's warm and I lay my cheek on his shoulder.

"So let's just take it easy and slow then," he suggests.

My comment has more to do with what I have to tell Robert than it does with Brody, but it comes none-theless, "None of this feels easy."

"It feels easy for me when I'm with you," he says and his admission is accompanied by a warmth that flows through my chest. "I think when you let me kiss you ... it's easy for you, isn't it?"

With my hand resting against his knee, my thumb rubbing back and forth along his jeans, I confess, "Yes. It's all easy when you kiss me."

"Let me take over then," he whispers and closes his eyes, leaning forward for a kiss.

"Wait," I say, barely getting out the word, remembering it was only one night ago that I was with Robert. Brody's eyes stare back at me, his body still as I tell him, "It's inappropriate."

A beat passes, only a single one before Brody lifts his lips in an asymmetric smile that puts me at ease, while simultaneously lighting my entire being on fire. "What part of me loving on my girlfriend is inappropriate?" he questions and my heart flutters like I've never felt. His gaze turns hot as he shifts me beneath him, his hand splayed on my back.

With my hands on his shoulders, he lowers me to the blanket and everything instantly burns with desire. My neck arches as his kisses trail down my throat.

"Brody." I moan his name and he lazily lifts his hooded eyes to mine.

"I love it when you say my name."

My heart pounds at the word love. He's said it twice tonight. I don't know if he's aware, but I am. Every detail of him, every word he says, every feeling that overwhelms me when I'm in his presence, it all brands itself into my memory.

He grabs my hand when I reach for his shirt, desperate to pull it off of him.

He tsks and says, "Not yet," then brings my knuckles to his lips. Kissing them one by one before telling me, "I want to take my time with you."

A sweet, desperate need lifts up my hips as I writhe under him. I'm met with a rough chuckle before his hand slips up my skirt, and then he cups me where I need him most.

He pauses for a moment, contemplating saying something. The hesitation is clearly written in his eyes.

"What?" I question, worried I've done something wrong or that last night has ruined the ease that was between us.

"Has Robert ever fucked you here?" he asks me, as his hand brushes against my ass.

A small gasp exposes my shock and I shake my head after slamming my lips shut.

"Good," is all he says and before I can question further, he moves and jostles my thoughts with his forceful touch.

His fingers press against my core and he rocks his wrist, sending pleasure to ebb and flow against my throbbing clit. My blood turns to a raging fire I can't evade.

Small moans slip past my parted lips and just as they escape me, I attempt to escape the pleasure that threatens to overwhelm me. Brody's large frame lowers, caging me in and holding me still beneath him. He nips the lobe of my ear and groans as his erection presses into my side, never letting up his ministrations.

Writhing under him, the pleasure builds and I bite down on my lower lip to stifle my moans. His fingers slip past the thin fabric that separates us and then dips into my heat. He's not gentle in the least, firmly stroking the most tender places, the rough pad of his thumb still rubbing ruthlessly at my swollen nub.

He captures my lips as I cry out his name and my orgasm crashes through me. Every inch of my skin tingles with a heat that's all too forbidden.

While I'm still falling and catching my breath, Brody undresses both of us. The gentle touch of his fingers caressing my sensitized skin prolongs the sensation. His hands are hot against me, his lips constantly kissing as he goes. I'm hardly aware that I'm nearly naked until the sound of my zipper fills the room. As he drags my skirt down my body, he licks from my navel downward.

My nails dig into his shoulders as he sucks my clit and then presses his tongue against it. My shoulders lift involuntarily as I cry out his name again, sucking in air before falling back down to the blanket.

It's all too much as another wave of pleasure builds,

this one stronger and more intimidating. He's relentless with his touch as he finger fucks me, dragging out the threat of another orgasm and I find myself begging him please, although I'm not sure for what.

To fuck me. To bring the impending orgasm to an end. My head is dizzy with lust and all I know is that I need him inside of me.

He lifts his head between my thighs to question, "Please, what?" The sight of him, licking my arousal from his lips, his masculine shoulders towering over me as he lifts himself to box me in … I'm overwhelmed by my attraction to him. So much so, everything seems to slow, to blur around him. The air bends to his will.

All I can say in response is an appeal. "Please, Brody."

Resting his forearms beside my head, he brings his lips to my ear at the same time that he presses himself against me, teasing my entrance. I wrap my legs around his hips, my heels digging into his ass as he whispers, "I wanted to take my time, but you make me a selfish man." With that, he slams himself inside me, all the way to the hilt, stealing the air from my lungs as he stretches and fills me.

My eyes are closed, my nails digging into his shoulders from the intense and sudden sting. The mixture of pain and pleasure taking me that much higher.

His groan of satisfaction is addictive as his warm

breath tickles my neck. His blunt nails dig into my hips as he holds me in place. "Bite down on my shoulder if you need to," he warns me, whispering just beneath the shell of my ear and kissing me there, in that tender spot.

I hardly register what he's said before he slams into me again, and again. Forcefully taking me, all the while I can't breathe.

He fucks me like he wants to ruin me, and it's everything I didn't know I wanted.

With every thrust, he fucks me harder, pistoning his hips ruthlessly until he finds his release at the same time that I find mine.

I'm breathless and trembling when he's done with me. My legs shake as he pulls out and the chill of the air replaces his warmth. He's quick to kiss me and I'm quicker to reach up, grabbing his stubbled chin and holding him there so I can kiss him deeper, praying that my kiss tells him everything I'm too afraid to say.

He takes his time, using the blanket to clean me up and then dresses himself. I'm slow to do the same.

"So what do we do from here?" Brody asks me once the moment is gone and pulls me into his lap. My hair is far from salvageable and all I can hope is that I don't look exactly like I feel: well fucked.

I nearly ask with what, then I remember everything else. The paternity test ... me telling Robert and then Bridget. I have no idea ... I wish I could give him the perfect answer. Instead my hand covers my eyes and I say, "If you're looking for answers from me, I can't give them to you. I barely have my own shit together."

"Did you just cuss?" he questions me with a devilish grin that's nothing short of handsome and a delighted tone. The heat in my cheeks rises higher from bashfulness as I hide my own smile. "That's the first time I've heard you cuss."

The tension eases, the nerves settle. It's so easy with him. How can it be this easy with a man who's lived his life without me in it? It still hurts to breathe, it still feels like I'm on the edge of falling and once the wind rushes beyond me, there's no going back.

He asks, "Will you at least let me kiss you?"

Closing my eyes, I lean forward and whisper against his lips, "I can do that."

CHAPTER
fourteen

Magnolia

THE PING OF MY PHONE ON THE COFFEE TABLE is barely heard over the sound of some cartoon playing on the TV in the background. Not that Bridget is watching it; she's having tea with Kitty. I should turn it off, but my mind has been elsewhere.

The delicate chime may as well be a fire truck siren since that's where my attention has been. Waiting for a text back from Robert.

Anxiety is my constant companion as I make my way from the kitchen to the living room. I plant my bottom down with disappointment onto the sofa as I read a text from my boss, a cup of coffee in one hand and my phone in the other.

I've never called out of work until this past month. This is the second time, but Mandy doesn't pry. Maybe she's too hungover, or maybe she knows I'm going through some things. I'm not certain, but I am grateful. Grabbing the remote, I turn off the TV and find myself staring back down at my phone like it's betrayed me.

I texted Robert that I want to talk to him. He saw the message, but didn't respond.

My heart knows that he knows, and it hurts. I won't pretend that it doesn't.

I don't want to be caught in the middle. I don't want to use either of them. I can list a million things I don't want, but the one thing I want isn't possible.

I want everyone to be loved and happy. Robert deserves that and it kills me that I can't provide it for him, when he's done that for me in my darkest times.

I've never considered it to be a possibility to be in love with two men at once. Or the idea of them at the very least. Maybe one is simply a best friend I can't live without, and the other a lover my heart recognizes as a necessity. That's the only explanation I have for why this aches like it does. I'm caught in limbo, conflicted and the dark hole I fell into years ago is trying to swallow me back up.

"Is that him?" Renee asks from where she's seated cross-legged on the floor, a plastic pink teacup in one hand.

"No," I answer while tossing both the phone and the remote back onto the coffee table. "I feel awful and stupid and like I can't do anything right."

Renee cuts in, "It's called dumb for dick … It's a real thing." She mouths the word "dick" and as if on cue, Bridget peeks up at her although Renee smiles innocently back.

A huff of a laugh turns genuine at my lips and it's the first laugh I've had today.

Ping. The semblance of a smile is quickly erased as I check the notification on my phone. My stomach drops and I freeze with my phone in my hand.

"You okay?" Renee doesn't hide her concern. "You just went pale all of a sudden."

The email is sitting right there and it's only a click away. Before I can answer her that the paternity test results are in, there's a knock at the door.

With my nerves plucking away at my rational side, I ask Renee, "Can you answer it?" My fingers hover over the inbox of my email. They're numb and refuse to press the button.

Every fear I've had ramps up, but they're all silenced by the sound of a familiar voice asking, "Is she here?"

I peek up to find Renee opening the door wider, her sorrowful expression seen before Robert steps inside.

"Bridge, do you want to build a playpen for Kitty in your room?" I ask my daughter, my heart racing. My hand trembles as I set the phone down, but other than that, I'm all smiles as I talk to Bridget. Renee helps me convince her to head to her bedroom.

"Thank you," I tell her and then stare back at Robert, who's a pitiful sight. Before I can say a word, my eyes fill with tears.

"Mags, please, don't." Standing there, whispering his plea, a man I know to be strong and capable drops to his knees. With both of his hands raised, his glossy eyes meet mine and he professes, "I love you."

With my hand over my mouth, I stifle back all my agony and make my way to him until I'm on the floor as well, my knees digging into the carpet and my hands over his. I can barely stand to look him in the eyes. His strong arms wrap around me and I rest my head on his shoulder. He does the same as he rocks me and kisses the crook of my neck. "I love you," he repeats. "I promised I'd love you forever."

Sobs wrack through me as my nails dig into his flannel shirt. "I think you wanted me to say more and I wish I had. I'm sorry." He barely gets out the words, but somehow he makes them sound strong. Pulling back, with both of his hands on my shoulders his pale blue eyes seek mine so he can tell me, "I'm sorry I didn't stay with you every night.

"I will make it all right. I will change. I will ..." he trails off, taking a moment with his eyes closed before opening them to peer back at me. "I didn't know what to do." He grieves our past in atonement. All the while he wipes under my eyes, rather than his own.

I confess, "I didn't know either."

That's the crux of our love. Life was brutal and we barely weathered it. Just kids moving through life with no guide, only leaning on each other in ways maybe we shouldn't have. At least we can say we did it with love. It left a tangled mess, but my heart knows it's true.

"I love you," I tell him, and sit back with my legs folded underneath me. There's hope in his eyes, until I finish and a piece of my heart begs me not to, but I have to. "But it's not fair to you, Robert."

"Don't," he begs me and I lay my heart bare.

"You were my first love—"

"Please, Mags." His head falls but I keep going.

"I love you, I always will, but it's a different kind of love. It's ours and no one can replace it, but it's not the same."

Inhaling a shaky breath, he respects the distance I put between us, inching back, but our hands are still entwined. His strong hands are now wrapped around mine. Even if they weren't, I wouldn't let his hands go. I grip them back just as much as he holds me.

"I know it's late to say it now. But if I could go back, I would change everything, Mags. I wish I could just go back." Swallowing thickly, he waits for me to say something, but I can't. Every word I know, every plea, every reason, every memory threatens to suffocate me if I dare speak. All I can do is shake my head, knowing how much I love Brody, how much loving him scares me, but how very real it is.

"Please, Mags …" His baby blue eyes are the epitome of sadness as he whispers, "I'm begging you."

A shuddered sob leaves me and all I can tell him is that I'm sorry. Steadying my breath, I lower our hands until he releases them and I cup his stubbled jaw, knowing it will be the last time. I don't dare kiss him. Even though he leans into my hand, closing his eyes. He takes it in his own and kisses the palm of my hand.

"I'll always love you," he whispers like it's a promise, and hot tears escape down my cheeks.

Licking the taste of salt from my lips, I selfishly try to lighten the moment with a whispered question. "Couldn't you make it easy on me and tell me you hate me?"

"I could never hate you, Mags." He gathers himself, seeming to take into account the fact that we're a mess on the floor. Pressing the heel of his palms to his eyes, he takes in a heavy breath. "I have to go," he says as he rises, but I stay where I am, merely watching him.

"I love you," he tells me again and I know he does.

I can't help but give him the truth back. "I love you too."

I watch him leave and the moment the door closes with a soft click, my body crumples forward and mournful sobs leave me. I'm still in that position when Renee comes out, asking me if I'm okay and I tell her the truth, I'm not.

I loved him. I still love him. I'll always love him.

But I love Brody more.

CHAPTER
fifteen

Magnolia

EVERYTHING IN MY LIFE MIGHT BE FALLING apart, but getting the results of the paternity test was supposed to make it a bit simpler. Not a thing feels easy about it after what I just went through. My eyes still burn and doubt fuels my anxiousness.

I've never been so thankful for Renee.

"I'm sorry you have to take care of this mess," I say, gesturing down the front of my pajamas for emphasis. My hair's still wet from the hot shower I just took.

Passing me two Advils, she orders me to take them to ward off the headache that comes from crying your eyes out.

"You'd do the same for me," is all she says and she's right. I would.

"You know you need to just open the email and get it over with, right? I think things will feel better once you do." She refers to the paternity test again.

Nothing feels easy or simple as I nestle into the couch with my throw blanket, along with the knowledge that the results are burning a hole in my phone.

Renee has been with me every step of the way so far. And clicking on this email will change my life, one way or another. More importantly, it will change Bridget's life. *Deep breaths.* I'm a good mama, and I have the best friends anyone could ask for.

With a dry throat I remind myself that's all that matters. This one email won't take that away. It may change things with Robert or Brody, but things have already changed.

Every time I consider ripping the bandage off, I can't get Robert's sorrowful gaze out of my head. He looked so devastated, coming here. I wanted to do better for him and take away his pain, and I couldn't do it.

Leaning my head back against the couch, I listen to the breeze blowing outside the window. The floor creaks as Renee steps away from Bridget's room before pausing in the hallway after putting the bottle back in the bathroom. My heartbeat is so loud.

Renee's footsteps approach the living room and I

open my eyes, parting my lips to tell her it's time to open the email. She interjects before I can say anything. "Convinced her to go down for a nap. You owe me one." I pat the couch next to me and Renee takes the spot I've offered. A crease forms in her brow. It's a change from how she seemed when she got up to get Bridget, but maybe she's just feeling the awkwardness from when Robert arrived. "I have to tell you something. It's something about Robert," she says with a long exhale.

At that moment, my finger slips. I don't mean to click the email, I just do. It opens, and the results are there on the screen.

"Robert is the father," Renee tells me with unexpected confidence. Her eyes are closed as if she's preparing to confess some sordid secret.

"What?" The word slips from me, my gaze moving from her to the phone.

I read the email twice in a row as the sound of her voice fades into the background. A numb sensation takes over my body, washing over me from head to toe. This moment has been a long time coming. My mind can't take it in, though.

Based on testing results obtained from the DNA analysis, the probability of paternity is 99.9999997%.

"He took the test years ago, when Bridget was

born." Renee's shaky voice cuts through my thoughts. Confusion comes along with her words. How could anyone have taken any test before? She's my daughter. "No." I utter the word softly, and Renee's expression sobers as she tells me, "I heard it from someone at the center. You know how people talk.

"It was too scandalous to keep to herself," she says then rolls her eyes and doesn't keep the distaste from her tone. As she carries on, I can't take my eyes off the phone and the words on the screen.

"He had the test done when she was born and he came that week, carrying all sorts of things for her. I was sure he was going to tell you, that he was going to step up and do the right thing."

I remember those days when Robert came to help me, and at those memories, more heartache overwhelms me.

"I'm sorry," she whispers. "If I could have helped you the way he had, I would have told you back then. But ... I couldn't and he was ... and ..."

"Renee, please," I mutter, closing my eyes and wishing it would all stop.

Renee touches my wrist. "He already knew he was the father. So don't feel bad about—"

"Brody's the father." The words leave me from numb lips. My throat's sore and tight, the words barely audible. I repeat, "Brody's the father. You're wrong."

"What?" Renee looks as confused as I feel. "No, Robert's the father. That's why he helped …"

"No. Brody is her father." I turn my phone to her so she can read the same words I just did. Brody's name is there in black and white. One question has been erased from my mind, but they've been replaced with more. "It's not Robert, it's Brody."

"I don't understand," Renee murmurs before she takes the phone from my hand. She holds it close to her face. The words won't change. I know, because I've read them ten times already. Brody's name is on those results.

Renee repeats with disbelief, "He took the test. I thought he only stayed because …"

"You thought he only helped me because he was the father?" With a wary expression, Renee nods. My heart breaks again. For me. For Renee. For Brody, who's going to learn he's Bridget's father, and for Robert, who has stepped up for my baby girl all these years.

Most of all, for my little girl. Robert's been there all her life. I have no idea what happens to us now.

"He helped me because he loved me," I tell her and wipe the tears from my eyes. "He's been in Bridget's life because he wanted to be." Every word hurts more and more. Peeking up at Renee, it's as if she doesn't believe it.

How could Renee not know what Robert and I were to each other? I can't comprehend how my best friend missed such a crucial detail.

"He loved me, Renee; I told you …"

The closeness I had with Robert isn't comparable to anyone else. He was my first love. In every way. I promised him under our oak tree that I would love him forever. My shoulders tense, bracing for another hit. I said those words to him, and I meant them.

"I thought he didn't want you to take the test because then he'd have to step up for real." Renee hands my phone back to me with a heavy sigh and regret shining in her eyes. "That's why I hated him so much." I'm not sure if her confession is meant for me or for herself.

Guilt tears through me again, bringing fresh tears to sting the corners of my eyes. "I wish you'd told me back then." My voice is soft as I tell her, careful not to make her feel any worse than she already does.

"I tried to tell you but the moment I was ready, you told me how much he was helping and giving you, and I couldn't replace what he was willing to give. Driving a wedge between that … I didn't know what would happen. I didn't want you to be worse off than you were and you … you were happy." Her eyes shine with tears as she tells me, "It had been so long since you'd been happy. I didn't want to take it from you."

I'm not angry with Renee. I know exactly how complicated things get when they involve other people. Especially people you love. I don't blame her for not coming to me with this news earlier, I just wish she had done it sooner. I wish I'd known. I wish Robert had told me.

Renee reaches for my hand. "I'm sorry. I didn't want to upset you."

"Everyone's trying not to upset anyone, but it's an upsetting situation, so …" A laugh slips out of me, but it's a painful one. How do things keep getting more tangled into knots? The more I find out, the less I know. It reminds me of the uncertainty I felt when I first discovered I was pregnant with Bridget. The hormones and emotions made for the perfect storm and I felt like I was losing my balance for months. The only thing that brought it back was Robert. And the times I thought about Brody. These two men are so entangled with my life.

And Bridget's … My own heart can break a million times, but I'm darn sure going to make sure I keep hers from getting broken along with it. Renee squeezes me before getting up to get tissues. She puts them in my lap and sits close by while I go through a third of the box, crumpling them up one by one as I look back on the last four years, imagining what Robert must've felt.

When my eyes are mostly dry, I look up at the ceiling and blink. "Okay. That hurt more than I thought it would."

"I'm sorry."

"It's a mess."

Renee snorts a little. "I would call it that, yeah." She continues watching me, running her hand through her hair nervously. All the times she was caustic when he was mentioned, I wondered why. Concern and apology shine in her eyes. Nothing can change the past, no matter how much you regret it. With a shaky breath I stand, and find my legs to be just as shaky.

"Where are you going?"

"I have to tell them." I should take my own advice and not spend so much time wishing I could change the past. "Well, maybe not Robert …"

My best friend shakes her head. "I imagine not. Since he's the one who already knows."

Renee stays quiet as I gather everything off the coffee table.

"Do you think you could watch Bridget for me?" I ask her.

"Yeah."

I bet it broke Robert's heart, learning he wasn't Bridget's dad. He never let on. All those times he came to my house and rocked her to sleep and played with her and saved me from breaking down, he knew. My heart aches with unconditional love for him.

"I'll tell Brody first. Then I'll talk with Robert."

"You want me to text them for you?" Renee's offer is as sincere as anything. She'd text anyone for me. Make any call I needed. Wouldn't be the first time either. "I'll rip the bandage off. I'll do it fast."

"I can do it." I take a long, deep breath. Time to live up to the mantras I keep repeating to myself. A good mama and a strong woman wouldn't shy away from doing what needs to be done. "They should also have the results by now, though. They know. If I know, they know." I should send something anyway, right? My fingers tremble as I reach for my phone. I'm not sure what to say to make this right with Robert. I'm not sure there's anything I can say to make it right. Sometimes you can't put broken things back together. "I'll message them. I need to grow up and do it."

"I think you've done a lot of growing up for a twenty-five-year-old," Renee says, pride in her expression. She adds, "Me growing up means buying Advil in advance for my hangover. Not … all this."

Brody is Bridget's father. I remind myself of the other half of this and it's … it's kind of perfect. Still, I struggle with it all.

"Why am I so sad?" I wish there were an answer she could give me that I'd accept, but there's not. There's not an answer in my heart, either, just a big, raw ache. "I didn't think it would hurt this much."

I'm not ready to meet this head-on. I know I need to explain things to Bridget. She's old enough to notice that all the other kids in her daycare have fathers, and I'll have to be honest with her. My baby deserves to know she has a father, and that I'm with him and I love him … but Robert.

"Sometimes I think it hurts so much because I'm not good enough for her." The truth slips away before I can stop it. Mama guilt is a real thing and rears its ugly head. "Maybe I'm not good enough for anyone, Renee. I feel like I don't deserve any love at all right now."

Renee leans in and looks me in the eye. "It's not about deserving love or being good enough. If you aren't allowed to make mistakes, we'd all be alone."

"I think I've made more than enough mistakes." I let myself laugh a little. It feels better than crying, though I still don't think much about this will ever be funny. "I'd like to do something right for once."

"Mama?" We both turn around and find Bridget in the doorway, her bedhead in a cloud around her face and her cheeks pink from a good long nap. I hold my arms out to her and she lazily makes her way to me, wrapping her arms around my leg. In the end, she'll be the most important person in my life. No question about that. No matter what happens, I have to do right by her.

"Look at your daughter," says Renee, reaching out to pat Bridget's hair. "If you ask me, you're doing great, babe. Just keep going."

CHAPTER
Sixteen

Robert

Three years ago

"**Y**OU LOOK GOOD WITH A BABY IN YOUR arms," I tell her, letting the words slip out. I didn't mean to, since it looks like sleep will take her any minute.

Magnolia's lips slip up into a beautiful smile, something I haven't seen her wear in far too long. "She's perfect," she murmurs. There's a darkness under her eyes that tells me she hasn't slept.

"Want me to hold her?" I offer. "I can take her if you want to go to bed."

"I'm here for that," Renee comments from the

kitchen and I look over my shoulder to find her drying a bottle with a towel. I make a mental note to bring dishcloths next time. The list of things Magnolia needs is entirely too long. But sleep is evidently the first item on that list.

"I forgot you were here," I say and grin at her, but she doesn't return the humor. There's a distrust in her glare I don't understand. We've always been friends.

"If you guys could," Magnolia says as she stands, the little one still firmly on her chest.

"Let me." I'm quick to help her up and then take Bridget from her. She's fast asleep, a delicate little bundle.

"I can—"

"It's fine," I say, cutting off Renee and remind her that my cousin had a baby last year. "I know what I'm doing," I add and again, Renee's response is cold.

My stomach drops, wondering if she knows. Bridget's only ten days old, and no one would know by looking, but she's not mine. Those little fingers that rest on my chest and the small coo as she wriggles into place … there isn't one bit that belongs to me.

She's not my daughter and judging by the way Renee reacts to Magnolia passing her infant to me, she knows.

"Just for a quick nap, then I'll try to pump again," Magnolia says but it's muddled with a yawn.

Magnolia offers me a simper, looking like she might say something else. It's hard to swallow as I wait to find out what it is. Especially with the shine in her eyes and that look of hers I know well. It's a look she used to give me back before this mess happened.

Whatever it is, though, she swallows it down, her gaze dropping to her stained nightshirt instead. "I should probably shower and change too," she comments with a hint of a laugh and then kisses the top of her little girl's head.

Before I can reply, Renee pipes in with, "You may feel better then." The tension between us only grows as I take my spot on the love seat, with Bridget resting, still sleeping, and Renee moves to sit on the chair across from me.

The floor creaks as Magnolia leaves us, saying, "Thanks, you guys."

"So, what have you been up to?" Renee asks me, and again her tone is off.

"Just work," I answer, searching her gaze for a hint of whatever she knows.

"She's having a rough time right now."

"I know."

It's so quiet, the click of the air coming on is the

only thing that can be heard. An anxious heat slips through me.

"I know what you did."

I don't answer at first, my lungs stilling and I wait for her to elaborate. There's so much I've done that's wrong, I don't know what she's specifically getting at. "Is that right?" I finally ask when she doesn't tell me what she's referring to.

"You waited to see if the baby was yours or not."

My hand instinctively splays across Bridget's back. She's so small, the span of my palm is larger than her back.

"You know you're the dad." Renee's sarcastic smile comes with a huff of ridicule. She doesn't know. It hurts to watch the disappointment shining back at me in her eyes. She swallows harshly, the sound filling the room. "You think occasionally letting her get a nap in is enough?"

I can't respond. Half of me wants to tell her the truth; the other half prays she'll tell Magnolia what she thinks. In the moment of silence, I imagine Magnolia coming to me, demanding for me to be here and to be in their lives. It would be perfect. She would let me love her again. If she thinks I'm the father, maybe she'd give me another chance. I would do it all right. I swear I would. Even if we are so young, I promise I'd be a good father.

In my absence of a response, Renee says, "You don't deserve her."

She's right. Renee is right. I don't deserve Magnolia. Here I am fantasizing about lying to her. To starting a life together built on lies. I don't know what's wrong with me or how I came to be the way I am. So much is wrong and I can't fix any of it.

It's so deceitful that everything Renee says makes me feel like this pain is deserved, even if she doesn't know the truth.

My phone chimes in the silence and as I shift Bridget to reach into my back pocket, Renee stands and takes her from me. "There, there, baby girl," she coos, cradling the little girl.

Her warmth is gone in an instant.

The text is from my father. "I have to go," I tell Renee, who doesn't respond. When my gaze moves from the message to her, I catch sight of her wiping tears from her face.

A vise tightens inside of me, making everything that's hurt violently scream in pain.

As I prepare to confess, she tells me, "Just go."

My throat is tight and it's all unforgiving as I quietly leave, hating that I can't face the truth, let alone share it with the people I care about. The door closes softly behind me and I breathe out a heavy exhale.

So?

185

So what? I respond. My father is the only one who knows. He pulled the strings to have the paternity test done.

About Magnolia's lawsuit.

What about it?

He questions, *Is she going to be able to come up with the money?*

I'm paying for it. Before my father can object, I add, *I'm not taking advice from you on this. She needs a good lawyer and we're going to make sure she has the best. Tell him I'll pay for it.*

She may never forgive me. I might never be able to make the last year we spent together as a couple right. But I can help her. I can fix the hell her father put her through. I can do the little things and be there. One day she might love me again.

The more whiskey I drink, the farther back the memories go. There are so many little details I missed, but somehow the bottle remembers.

The bark against the oak tree at my back seems to soften. The breeze turns colder as the night sets. If I wasn't so stiff, I'd get my ass up and find somewhere else to spend my evening.

But I don't want to go home and see my mother.

I don't want to go to my apartment that's cold and empty.

I don't want to go anywhere but backward in time.

The taste of the whiskey reminds me of one of our first kisses after Bridget was born, on the back porch of my parents' house. She came by to drop something off. I was half a glass in and offered her the remainder.

Whiskey never tasted so good as it did lingering on her lips, her hands resting on my shoulders. As I deepened our kiss, her nails scratched their way down my back and she straddled me.

If I could go back, I don't know which time I would pick. I love her, but Bridget … the world wouldn't be right without her little girl.

Footsteps alert me to the fact that someone's coming and through gritted teeth I suck in a breath, wiping under my eyes and pulling myself together. My back aches as I try to stand and the world tilts slightly, the bottle sloshing in my hand.

"Don't get up," a voice says, firm but not confrontational.

I still where I am, a prick traveling down my neck.

"Brody." I deserve a fucking award for not saying his name like the curse it is. It took me a long time to not blame him for everything. I know it was my fault, I started it all, but if he hadn't been there …

"Robert." Brody mocks the way I say his name, but there's a friendly grin on his face and he's quick to take a seat next to me, facing the same dimming sunset sinking into the sea on the horizon.

"What are you doing here?" I question him.

"I was asking for you at your office, and the girl at the front said sometimes you take your lunch down here.

"It's quiet," Brody comments and then his gaze falls to the bottle in my hand. He rights himself, staring at the water. "So I can see why you like it."

"Yeah … the quiet is good sometimes," I say, just now realizing I'm more drunk than I'd like to be. In the far distance, kids can be heard playing sometimes. There's a park behind a row of trees to the right. But other than that, it's just the sound of the ocean and the kiss of the autumn breeze.

I nearly tell him about this tree. About the promise I made her. The words scream inside, wanting to tear their way up my throat so he'll know. I want him to know exactly what he took from me. But if a single word comes out, I know I'll lose it. More than that, I know I'm the one to blame.

"Thanks for signing over the approval for

everything," Brody says and I stare at him. The longer I stare, the more I see Bridget and my gaze falls.

"Why are you here?" is the question I settle on after a moment passes.

Anger bristles inside of me, but he doesn't share the sentiment.

"I thought we should have a," he takes in a breath, waving his hand in the air like he's searching for the right word, "a second chance at meeting one another."

Fuck you. The words are right on my tongue, but I bite them back. If I have any chance at staying in their lives, I know I'm going to have to deal with him.

"I was going to pressure you. I was going to deny every form you ever submitted." The confession slips out honestly. I didn't even mean it to. The pain of why I didn't is just too much to hold in.

"Well, that would have been awful dickish of you," Brody comments and his elbow hits my arm. When I look back at him, he motions to the bottle. My gaze narrows and he says, "Come on, man."

A second passes before I hand him the bottle and he takes a swig. He hisses out after taking a gulp of it. Holding it out in front of him he comments, "You couldn't get anything better?" His eyes are wide and an honest chuckle leaves me.

"Burn too much for you?" I question while taking the bottle back. This bottle is meant to hurt on the way down. If he really loved Magnolia, he'd know that.

"I know you're pissed, but damn ... you don't need to pile on the misery."

"It's not—" I start to tell him, then shake my head, feeling an emptiness deep inside that swallows up the words.

"What?"

"You won't understand," I say and then untwist the cap, but he takes the bottle from me.

"Tell me," he asserts. "I want to know. Tell me."

The sincerity of it is what breaks me. He wants to know?

"You don't know the hell we went through," I barely speak the words and then breathe out. The agony of it all swarms inside of me and I expect to see hate, disgust, or a holier-than-thou expression staring back at me, but all I see is him nodding. "I have a lot to catch up on," he tells me.

"It's not for you to know."

"Well, if you want to tell someone, I'm here." He swirls the whiskey and then stares down the neck of the bottle like he might take another swig, or he might not.

It's the knowledge that I'm at his mercy that leads me to tell him. "I don't want to drag Magnolia into anything. I just want to be there." The idea of not being able to talk to her, especially now, with my mother, with Bridget growing up … I just can't comprehend what it would do to me. I don't think Magnolia would choose to go that route. "She's always been my best friend," I tell him and then feel like a prick, pinching the bridge of my nose. There's got to be a better word for it. *Best friend* isn't good enough.

"You might hate me, but I don't hate you." Again, Brody's voice is easygoing. I don't trust him.

"Why is that?"

"You took care of my daughter," he says simply and I'll be damned if it doesn't hurt all over again. My throat's dry as I rip my gaze away and stare at the waves that rush against the shore.

"Fuck, dude," Brody murmurs. "I'm sorry."

"They are my family," I comment and reach for the bottle, only to find it empty.

"You dumped it?" My accusation is met with a blank gaze.

He looks me dead in the eye and lies, "Nah, I'm a manly man and I chugged it."

I can't help the crack of a laugh that leaves me.

"Liar," I say and he only laughs.

After a second, I laugh with him. He's got a good sense of humor. I see why Magnolia likes him. At that thought, the glimmer of a smile fades from my lips.

A manly man. I stare down at the empty bottle in my hand. I don't feel like much of a man at all right now.

He clears his throat and says, "You need good shit. Not ... this."

I can only murmur a noncommittal response.

"I just wanted to come down here and tell you, thank you."

"I don't fucking like this. It feels like the end and it can't be." I repeat to him, emphasizing the plea in my tone, "They're my family."

"I wouldn't do anything to keep them from you."

"You say that, but ..." Again, I don't trust him.

"I don't think Magnolia would like it if I did." He says the statement without judgment and I peer at him as he stands up, brushing the dirt from his pants.

"I'm not perfect, and she's not mine the way she is yours. But I'm not going to let you come in and erase me." As I stand, I check my phone and find it dead. Dammit. Nothing can go right this week.

"I don't intend to. I'm asking you, though, for Magnolia's sake, I need you to give her time."

"For Magnolia's sake," I echo his words and sneer.

"I mean it. And I think you know she needs it."

Staring at this man from his work boots, up his jeans to the dark gray Henley, I look him right in the eye. As I'm about to question him on what he could possibly know about what Magnolia needs, he says,

"It's not a fight. It's not a game of tug-of-war. You're her friend, and I want to be her husband. It doesn't have to be anything more than that. Don't make it something it's not."

Brody

Robert is wrecked.

I feel bad for him. He seems like a good guy. That makes sense, since Magnolia loved him.

I have to remind myself that it's in the past. Past tense. Loved.

Although the messages Renee sent Griffin are less than ideal.

She's wrecked too.

I knew Bridget was mine. Getting that email and then a text from Magnolia only confirmed what I already knew was true. She's my baby girl and I've missed so much. How I wound up here rather than at Magnolia's is simple.

Renee told Griffin I needed to give Magnolia time. Because of Robert. It's far easier to confront him than it is to wrap my head around the fact that I have a little girl in my life forever now. It would be damn easier, though, if it'd gone like I expected it to. Which is not at all like this.

"You need a ride home?" I offer him as he chucks the bottle into a trash bin on the sidewalk by the shore. His back is to me, but he stops. He's not holding his liquor well and judging by the direction he was heading, it wasn't to the parking lot.

"Can I just use your phone?" he asks me and braces himself on the wood of the pier. "I'll call my friend for a ride."

"I can drive you," I say and he shakes his head. "You really want to walk home like that?" I gesture to his tie that's undone. "Your face is red, especially your …" I take a deep breath, debating on whether or not I should point it out. His eyes are red rimmed. If he makes a right at the end of the block where other people are, they're going to know he was crying at the very least. There's nothing worse than a grown man crying … other than one who's also drunk before 2:00 p.m.

"I need to learn the layout anyway," I comment and pull out my keys, letting them jingle in my hand.

"You really aren't going to let me use your phone?"

"No. Tell me where to take you. I insist." Robert stares at me as he undoes the rest of his tie and pulls it off entirely. "Let me do something nice, for fuck's sake."

"If you just take me up a few blocks," he says, relenting slightly.

I didn't anticipate it going down like this. In my mind, he'd punch me, he'd threaten me. I thought he'd tell me that the moment I screwed up, he'd be there for her.

Instead, all I see is a man afraid to lose the people he loves.

Which is exactly what Renee told Griffin. Magnolia loves Robert, but it's as a friend.

It's hard to swallow, but it's not like either of us is going anywhere any time soon.

The chill in the air is worse now than it was when I got here an hour ago. I spent a good twenty minutes just watching Robert.

I glance at him as he closes the passenger door, the somber expression still present. "You said a couple blocks up?" I ask as I slip the key into the ignition and turn the engine over. The sight in front of me is beautiful, the sunset over the water by the dock.

Something stirs inside of me, imagining Magnolia and I walking down the pier, each holding Bridget's hand and swinging her as we make our way to the water. It feels like home. Like it was supposed to be.

"Yeah, to, uh, I think you met Asher?"

My brow pinches as I try to remember. "Yeah."

"If you could take me to his shop, that's far enough."

A number of questions hit me and they must be written on my face, because he explains, leaning his head back against the headrest, "I just want to crash there is all."

"Whatever you want, man." As I respond, Robert rolls the window down, closing his eyes and letting the breeze hit him. I imagine he's trying to stay awake. He had to have drank half that damn whiskey. When he pinches the bridge of his nose, I know he's crying again.

Why couldn't he just be a prick?

Debating whether or not I should make a joke about not getting sick in the truck, I watch him stare out the window while telling me it's just five blocks up, make a right and it's the hangar down the road. All the while he pretends he's not crying. So I don't say shit. I give the man space.

I wish I had something more to say to him, but I'm not sure he's in the right mind to hear it anyway, so I turn up the radio and we drive in silence.

As we get to the first red light on Main Street, he catches me off guard with a comment spoken so low I don't know if he meant for me to hear it or not. He drunkenly slurs, "How did I ever stand a chance? You're Bridget's dad. You didn't fuck up. She was never going to pick me."

The music and the window being down didn't help to keep him awake, though. By the time I get to the hangar, ten minutes later, Robert is passed out.

Luckily, Asher's standing out in front of his shop

and sees. At first his gaze was questioning. The moment of clarity is quickly followed by a downcast look.

"You doing all right?" he asks me as I turn off the truck and he approaches. His gaze slips right by me to Robert.

"He asked to come here," I tell him although my tone implies it's a question.

"You kick his ass?" Asher asks and judging by the look on his face, he's serious. There's not a hint of emotion there, it's just him wanting to know.

In my silence, he questions, "Or is … did he have a little too much?"

"A little," I say, finally opening my door, and get a gust of fresh air. I make my way around to the passenger side with Asher as he tries to wake Robert up, but it's not happening.

"You get his legs, I get his arms?" I offer and Asher nods.

"You tell anybody?" he asks me as he opens the door up as wide as it can go.

"No."

He gives me an expression I can't place; some part defensive, some part hurt. "Could you not? If it could stay between us, I'd appreciate it."

"I don't plan on telling anyone." Griffin doesn't even know I'm here. No one knows, and no one has to.

"Magnolia?" he asks.

"I'm not going to lie to her, but I don't have to tell her."

"Good, good," he mutters and inhales deep before grabbing his half of Robert's limp frame.

"Shit," I curse through gritted teeth as I help carry him inside. There's a room in the back of his shop and as I take a look around, it reminds me of a hangout Griffin and I used to have.

"You—"

"It's for him."

I have to take a second to puzzle out what Asher just said. "For Robert?"

"Look, I know you don't owe me anything. But … he hasn't been doing well with family things. His mom's not well."

"So he comes here?"

"He hasn't wanted to be alone. And with you," he gestures, "he didn't want to put stress on Magnolia, going over there and 'bringing her down,' as he put it."

I stand there, not knowing what to say other than, "I don't really know anything about him."

"He's a good man, a good friend of mine. He's … shit, he's fucking rock bottom." Asher looks at his friend sleeping on an unmade bed and then back to me before saying, "He's going through a lot, and I'd appreciate it if you didn't hold whatever he's said or done against him. I know you and Magnolia … I know you two are together."

"I love her."

Asher nods, motioning to the front of the shop where a porch wraps around the side. It's obviously a newer addition. "You want a drink, lover boy?" he jokes and then smiles. Now he's much more like the first version I met of him. Light and funny.

"I should get back I think," I tell him, feeling out of place and honestly like shit after seeing the state Robert's in. I turn toward my truck, still parked out front but his voice stops me.

"You know … I just want to say," Asher tells me, turning serious again. "And I'm only telling you because I believe you when you say you love her. And Robert's my friend."

"I get that," I say and nod, squaring my shoulders as I face him.

"His mom, Robert's mom, she has good days."

"Good days?"

"She didn't tell you?"

"Magnolia? She didn't tell me anything about him. I didn't ask." Asher takes a moment, seeming to ponder over whatever he was thinking.

"She has Alzheimer's that's just gotten worse over the years."

"Shit, I didn't know. I'm sorry."

Asher waves it off as he walks over to the edge of the porch railing and leans against it. I follow him, joining in looking out into the thicket of trees.

"I've known her all my life. When my dad was having moments, I'd go hide out over at his place and vice versa," Asher says. He blows out a breath and then crosses his arms over his chest. "I came with him a few times, but it's hard …" he looks at me to add, "seeing her like that, you know?"

"Yeah, I get it," I tell him although I've never gone through such a thing. I can imagine, though, and it only adds to the mournful mood.

"She told Robert once, one time when she was more with it and remembered who he was, that Magnolia would never love him the same way. They were star-crossed lovers and he'd already had a chance to love her, and he needed to let her go."

Shit. I look down at my boots, not wanting to imagine that.

"I think it fucked him up real good," Asher comments and then pats the railing of the porch. "Like I said, he's a good guy, he's just had a real hard time and he's shit at dealing with it."

I nod in understanding and struggle to find something to say in return. "He's going to have one hell of a hangover to add on top of it all."

Asher huffs out a laugh. "A couple Advil and he'll

be all right. Don't let me keep you," he tells me and then adds, "If you need anything, I'm here."

"Thanks." I give him a wave and stop myself from turning around before adding, "Same to you. If you need anything, or if ..." I can't help but to add, "If there's anything I can do to help him."

"He'll be all right. It'll take more than two pills, but he'll be all right."

CHAPTER
Seventeen

Magnolia

C ALM COMES AFTER A STORM. THAT'S WHAT people say, and it's true.

For a long time I thought I'd never feel settled, never feel whole again. It didn't seem possible for me with everything that happened four years ago. The scandal my dad caused … Finding out I was pregnant … Moving home again only to feel it was nothing like home at all anymore.

I thought it would just keep raining and always be gray skies I learned to deal with.

It still feels like a storm after telling Robert it's over; I don't know that the pain will ever really leave. My eyes still burn with all the tears I've shed. It was never supposed to end this way with Robert. It was never supposed to be this painful. But that's the thing about storms. You can't stop them from coming. You just have to ride it out.

Taking a deep breath, I close my eyes then pull the sheet and comforter up to my neck and let my heartache take me to sleep. It's a clear night, but soon I hear the patter of rain on the roof. After a few minutes it's coming down in buckets. *When it rains, it pours.* That's what they say, right? Maybe I was wrong about the calm after the storm. If the calm was before the storm, I'm in trouble.

It takes hours for me to actually sleep. Regret keeps me up, reminding me of all the mistakes I've made. A few times I glanced at the clock, reading 1:00 a.m., 2:00 a.m. … and then I just stopped looking. Eventually, though, I fall into a deep, dreamless sleep. When I wake up, Bridgey's standing at the side of my bed, staring at me. "Mama, it's morning," she whisper-shouts, in the way kids do. I can't help but to smile at her chubby little cheeks as I cup her face.

My heart may hurt forever, but it's filled with love forever too.

"It's morning?" I question her as if that's not obvious. The light's peeked in from my blinds and the clock reads it's already after eight.

"Look," she says and points to my window, "the sun's awake."

With a grin, I nod my head and stretch as I sit up in bed. "You're right about that, baby."

My eyelids are puffy from all the crying and my heart still aches, but other than that … I'm okay. I feel washed clean, in a way. Just like I would if I stood out in those buckets of rain I heard and let it rinse the pain away.

Climbing out of bed, I lead Bridget out of the room with a pat on her back, listing all the fun things we can do today, and head into the kitchen.

"Want to help me make coffee?" I offer her. She enjoys doing the "adult things," so of course she nods vigorously. Sitting her on the counter, she heads right for the coffee filters.

"I know what to do," she tells me and my confident little girl gets going while I do my best to keep smiling for her. We count the scoops of coffee together.

With each scoop, I try to ignore the hammering of thoughts in the back of my mind. I don't want the past to be cleared away, or anything like that. I would never want to forget Robert. How could I ever forget him?

Ping. My phone goes off just as Bridget is stirring in creamer.

"Down you go," I tell her and she runs off to go play after I promise to make her pancakes.

It's a message from Brody. My smile comes easier reading such a little thing: *Good morning, beautiful.*

Just thinking of Brody makes my heart hum in this delicious way. I make the pancakes I promised, texting him all the while.

He makes me smile. He makes me laugh. He makes me want to share everything with him … except the thoughts of Robert.

With a burst of courage, I ask him if he wants to go to lunch. It seems like the perfect way to mark the occasion, which is that we're together. Together, together. I wonder if it'll feel like a special occasion forever.

I hope it does.

Are you asking me out on a date? he texts and I huff a small laugh.

"What's funny?" Bridget questions me, a chunk of pancake speared on her fork.

I wonder what she'll think of him. There are so many obstacles still to come.

I'm going to take Bridget out, I message Brody. *So it'll be the three of us for lunch.*

He was so careful around Bridget when I made lasagna. He was quiet, awkward even but then again, so was I. This morning enough weight has been lifted from my shoulders to step into the next part of this. Bridget needs time to meet her father and really get to know him, and Brody needs time with her too. Not with Renee and Griffin. Today is as good a day as any, if he's up for it.

He's more than up for it. Brody messages back without letting a second pass that of course, wherever we want to go is fine. There's an undertone of affection with his message that heats up my chest. *Taking my two ladies out to town sounds like the perfect way to spend the day.*

We have a morning of cartoons during which my mind is occupied with a million possibilities, and then we pick out "almost matching" blue dresses to wear, according to Bridget. Technically she's in a Snow White dress and I'm wearing a simple navy number, but I go along with what she says and we head downtown to meet Brody. The Blue Sail is a place we don't go often, but I know Bridget loves the menu and they have little coloring books that will keep her butt in a seat longer than other places.

Normally, I have to eat quickly, but for this ... I want us to have time.

My heart picks up the moment I see him, as if it's racing me to the restaurant. Brody is waiting for us out front on the sidewalk in a pair of jeans and a white button-down that makes his tanned skin seem even tanner. The sight of him makes my heart go pitter-patter. He has the sleeves rolled up to his elbows and looks so perfectly casual and strong. Stubble that leaves a light burn on my skin when we kiss covers his chin.

But the best part is the way his whole face lights up when he sees us. "You look beautiful." He bends down and kisses my cheeks, and Bridget pulls on my hand.

"Am I beautiful?" she chimes in, twisting on her feet a bit.

Brody's eyes go wide. "The most beautiful little princess I've ever seen."

Brody's eyes follow every movement of her face as Bridget lifts a pudgy hand to touch his chin. "You're poky." She scrunches up her nose and he laughs. His laugh makes her smile, her biggest grin, and the three of us go into the restaurant floating on that feeling.

It's just too good to be true. Nervousness makes me feel like the other shoe is bound to drop.

It gets more real as we take a booth in the front. Bridget tucks herself in by my side and Brody sits across from us. "My mom's headed to the airport today." Brody looks into my eyes although his fingers fidget with the napkin wrapped around the silverware, and I see more of that guarded longing. He wants this as much as I do. "She'll want to meet Bridget before she goes."

My heart slams up into my throat. It's nerve wracking, getting what you want. It's painful and strange and exciting. Being with Brody is going to mean letting new people into Bridget's life, starting today. "Did you tell her?"

"Not yet, but I want to ask her to come down later … if you're all right with that."

Before I can answer, he stumbles over his next words. "I just feel like it wouldn't be right to not tell her."

"Of course," I reply, but I have to clear my throat and repeat myself. "Of course she can come." At that moment, Bridget drops a sugar packet and I bend to pick it up, taking a moment to calm myself down as he texts his mother.

The anxiousness is in full force, my nerves running a mile a minute.

The waitress swings by and drops menus onto the edge of the table. "Can I get everybody something to drink?"

"Chocolate milk for this one," I answer automatically, "and an iced tea for me, please." Brody orders a Coke, and when the waitress bustles away I turn back to him and tuck an arm around Bridget.

"Where did you want your mom to meet her?" I ask him, barely able to breathe at the thought. I'm caught up in him. I'm caught up in them … adding another person, another change. It feels so fast.

"Down here?"

"Down to where?" My mind's not fully grasping what he's saying.

"To here, the restaurant. She already ate, or—"

Oh, no. "Did you already eat?" I say, cutting him off

without meaning to. The rain-washed feeling from this morning is wearing off. Couples talk over each other and negotiate and screw up. It's one thing to fantasize about a person. It's another thing to be muddling through a shared life with them. Then again, Brody is a fantasy all by himself.

His expression turns sheepish. "I ate, but—"

"I'm sorry. If I'd known—"

"Like I was going to say no." His smirk is comforting. "You can relax, I can always eat." He reaches across the table and his strong hand covers mine. Brody's skin is always warm, and I can feel the calluses left from his years of hard work. "I've been dying to see you guys anyway." He pauses and seems to consider something before adding, "Any time I can get with her, really. I know I've missed a lot and I don't know the best way …"

His voice trails off and I don't know the right words either, but I know what he's getting at so I simply answer, "I know."

The waitress comes by again and this time she drops a paper place mat with a bucket of crayons and a sheet of stickers for Bridget. My baby girl is up on her knees right away, digging through the bucket and picking out her favorites. She's so serious about it. Her tongue sticks out from between her teeth as she draws. Her scribbles are serious art and the stickers, she says, are the price tags. "I could sell that in the gallery," I tell her, kissing the top of her head.

Brody watches her color with the same attentiveness he had the other night. I'm caught off guard when he asks, "You think she'll call me Dad?"

My throat goes tight with emotion, but the rest of my body goes stiff. I've been responsible for keeping Bridget safe since the day she was born. Since before she was born, actually. I don't know why Brody's question makes that protective instinct flare up in me.

Well ... yes I do. It's because I know how it feels to have a man walk out of your life. On top of that, I know how it feels to have your own dad turn out to be a totally different person than you thought he was. I don't want that for Bridget.

His baby blue eyes stare back at me, vulnerable and sincere. My heart pounds, reminding me of what's between us and that even if it's scary, that raging storm and chaos I feel around him is because I'm falling for him. I have fallen for him already.

Love is scary. But if another person can love my daughter the way I do, I want that for her.

I take a deep breath to calm the pounding in my veins. "She's your daughter, so ... whatever you like."

"I'll leave it up to her." Brody clears his throat, and I can see him trying to keep his emotions in check. She is his baby girl too, and he's missed out on most of her life so far. We're just out to lunch at a restaurant I've been to a hundred times, but this time is different. It has a feeling to it that I can't place. It's hard to breathe, wanting everything to go perfectly.

Bridget sticks her tongue between her lips and blows a raspberry.

"Bridgey," I scold, laughing. "Not in the restaurant."

She giggles at me, tossing her head back which makes her laugh sound even louder. I catch Brody's eye over her head. He doesn't hold my gaze for very long because he's too busy looking at her. Our daughter. I'm not sure why I tense up when he inches closer to connecting with Bridget. The truth is that she wouldn't exist without him. If I hadn't met this gorgeous stranger in the bar that night, I wouldn't have my Bridget.

Bridget draws a fat red line across her paper. Her head pops up, and I know instantly she wants Brody's approval.

"What do you think?"

"It's stunning," he says with his brow raised and then smiles back at her. It's almost overwhelming how natural it feels.

"Are you ready to order?" Margorie, our waitress with tight red curls, startles me and Brody smiles at my yelp. His laid-back attitude eases something in me.

I let out a small laugh and nod. "I think we're ready. You?"

"Yeah," Brody agrees, "we're ready."

Scanning us all carefully, probably for tidbits of gossip, the waitress leans in and takes our order.

As soon as she's gone again, Brody settles back into his seat. "Is mac and cheese her favorite?"

"Always. Anything pasta," I answer him.

"I love berries too. Strawberries," she says with a little kid slur. "Blueberries, raspberries."

"Yes, she does," I say and nod in agreement, smiling at my little girl.

"Berries, got it. What else should I know?" he asks her, genuinely engaging her in conversation and I can't help how I feel. I love him even more.

So many things had to happen for the two of us to be sitting across from each other in this booth.

It's beginning to feel like it was supposed to happen this way with Brody. We had to meet in the bar by chance that night four years ago. I had to make my way back home to this town. And he had to make his way here too.

It's not until our meals are here that I ask him a question I've been wondering since the moment I saw him on the patio at Charlie's Bar and Grill weeks ago. "What made you come here?"

Brody rubs his knuckles against his chest, a sad smile curving his lips. "My grandfather talked about this place. He …" His sentence trails off, but he might as well have continued speaking for all the love in his voice. "I liked to listen to his stories, and he mentioned it one time. Visiting the places he talked about makes it feel like he's still close by. Plus, Griffin grew up near here, so it was a bit of a homecoming for him too."

Tears sting my eyes and emotions swell like the tide coming in. Brody and I have had threads connecting us running through our lives for longer than we've known. It doesn't seem like a coincidence that we ended up here together. "I'm glad you came."

"Me too," Brody tells me, a half grin on his face like this is no big deal. Like our lives aren't changed forever … and for the first time in so long, for the better.

CHAPTER
Eighteen

Magnolia

I CAN'T SAY IT SURPRISES ME WHEN BRODY doesn't want our lunch date to end. He has asked Bridget practically a million questions, and she's asked him that same number times two.

By the time we finish our lunch, followed by root beer floats —a true treat for my little one—Bridget is on his side of the booth. She draws something unrecognizable, saying it's Kitty's house, shows it off to him, then colors some more. It's a dream come true, seeing them together like that. Father and daughter sit side by side. Brody is a strong, calm presence, and Bridget is light and free.

This is how it's supposed to be. I still have that feeling, though, like the other shoe is going to fall.

I'm also far too aware that his mother is going to come by at some point.

"We should probably get going," he comments, checking his phone after paying the bill. I wish I could see the texts, my curiosity rampant at wondering what his mother is like ... it's all so nerve wracking.

"She should be here soon, though." He swallows thickly.

"How soon?"

"Like an hour?" he guesses.

"We don't have to go home," I proclaim, needing fresh air myself.

"She could meet us at the park?" I offer and he nods away, texting his mother to do just that.

It's then that I get a message, and then another.

"Brody, how about you and Bridget head to the playground for a bit?" There's a small, but really nice playground next to the public library just down the block. Bridget likes to play there when I have time, which hasn't been often enough lately.

"Just us?" he questions and I don't know if there's a sense of fear there or surprise.

"I'll stand back a bit ... I have a little something to do, if you don't mind. And it'll let you have a moment

215

with her," I tell him although it comes out as half a question.

"You'd be okay with that?" Brody arches an eyebrow at me, looking so hopeful it squeezes my heart. "What is it you need to do?"

There is something important I need to do. If there's anything my life has taught me, it's not to leave things unresolved with people. That's a good recipe for losing them entirely.

"I think I have something I have to tell someone," I say and then close my eyes, hating that for even a second I considered keeping it from Brody. My fingernails dig into my palm and I swallow down the fear of what being honest could do to us. "I want to reach out to—"

"Robert?" he guesses and although there's a flash of uncertainty in his gaze, when I nod, he nods in return.

"Is it okay?" I ask him.

"Yeah, I get it," he answers and those nervous butterflies rev up in the pit of my stomach. He doesn't ask me what I need to say. He doesn't ask me anything at all.

"It shouldn't take long. If you're up for this, I mean. If you're not—"

"I am." He cuts me off with a masculine confidence that sends shivers down my spine. Brody pulls back, his face softening. "I mean, I'm more than good. What do you like to do at the playground, Bridget? Swings? Merry-go-round?"

"Swings," she tells him, abandoning her crayons on the table in front of her. "I want to go on the swings."

"It's settled, then." We make our way out of the restaurant and into the golden afternoon sunlight. It's one of my most favorite times of day, when there's still enough daylight left for seemingly infinite possibilities. I pull Bridget in for a hug. "Go to the playground and have fun, okay? I'll be right there."

Bridgey squirms out of my arms and goes straight to Brody. He laughs, surprised, but he holds her hand like he's done it for years. "Tell your mama goodbye." He can't wipe the grin off his face when he says the words. His voice brings a new depth to them.

My daughter waves to me and twists in Brody's grip. "Playground," she says. "I want to go on the swings."

"Your wish is my command," Brody tells her, and he swings her up onto his shoulders. Oh, goodness. Maybe I should buy stock in tissues. I could cry all the happy tears right now.

I watch Brody and Bridget walk away together until they cross the street, and then I pull out my phone. The answer doesn't take long to come.

Robert's waiting for me at the corner of the park ten minutes later. He looks put together and professional, the way he always does when he's working. This is who Robert is. He drops everything to meet me whenever I ask him.

"Hey, Mags." He greets me with his hands in his pockets, a nervous look in his gaze. "I'm surprised you wanted to talk."

"I couldn't leave things with you the way we left them the other night. Not after everything we've shared."

Cool breezes move under the canopy of leaves that haven't already started to turn to shades of auburn, surrounding us like an old friend. We've stood here so many times before. "I wanted to say—"

Robert cuts me off with a wave of his hand. "Let me go first. There's—there's something I need to get off my chest."

Emotions threaten to overwhelm me again, bumping together until they're tough to name. Fear at what he might say. Sorrow that it didn't work between us after all. I'm grateful we're having this conversation. I'm relieved and nervous all at once.

"I didn't want to break up with you." Robert looks me square in the eye.

"What?" I can't disguise the surprise in my tone.

He continues. "Back then, when it all …"

I try to stop him, his name a plea on my lips, but he says, "Please, I just have to tell you."

With a nod of understanding, I let him get out what he wants, and then I'll get out what I need to.

"It was my father's idea. He stood over me while I was on the phone with you to make sure I didn't back out. And Mags, I shouldn't have. I should have told you beforehand that it wasn't me, and I didn't want it."

My throat goes so tight it aches, remembering how it felt to have that call years ago but I swallow down the urge to become emotional. I've had enough of that already.

"I'm not sure what I should say." Comforting him still feels like the right thing to do, but I'm not sure if I'm the right person to do it.

"You don't have to say anything, Mags," Robert tells me, running a hand through his hair. "I just wanted you to know."

Anger tightens my chest. Or is it just sadness that we couldn't have been more honest before?

"I have something to get off my chest too," I admit to him. "You knew you weren't Bridget's father. You never told me, and you know I spent so many nights—"

He looks away. "You don't understand, I didn't want it to be true."

"Didn't want what to be true?" I get that he must've been hurt, but it's no excuse. Frustration rises up in me and I take a deep breath to try and calm it down. "Explain it to me. I'm here to listen."

He runs both hands down his face and drops them back to his sides. "You weren't supposed to come back," Robert clarifies. "That week, when things were exposed, you weren't supposed to be here."

"I didn't want to." There's some honesty. My real feelings come through loud and clear in my voice. "I came back because my dad died."

"I didn't know."

"Didn't know what?"

"I didn't know you'd come home and put yourself in the middle of everything with your dad." Robert's eyes meet mine and I see his anguish at the surface. He gets it under control, though. He doesn't let it take over. "I thought you would stay away. Anyone would have stayed away from that mess, and then there you were. It made it so damn hard to—" He shakes his head, anger radiating from him. I can see it's an old wound. About as old as mine. "My plan was to wait until the scandal died down and then beg you, on my goddamn knees, to take me back. My name wouldn't be associated with the scandal, you'd be out of it too and your father would have to deal with the mess he made alone.

"There wasn't a moment I didn't love you," Robert confesses. "But you came back and you sure as hell didn't love me anymore. Everything was … nothing went the way it was supposed to. So I—" His voice breaks, and my heart breaks along with it. "I gave you space. I did whatever you told me to do, but I …"

"You shouldn't have tried to—" I can barely speak, thinking about all the pain of that year.

"I know," is all he says. "I just wanted you to know."

"And the paternity test?"

"I love you, Mags. I wanted it not to be true, so I didn't tell you." Rustling leaves from the tree fall and scatter, making small noises onto the grass around us. "I didn't know what to do, and I was young and dumb. I thought if I waited, you'd want me back one day." He swallows thickly. "I made a lot of mistakes and the more time that passed, the less I felt like I could tell you any of it. The more I blamed myself."

"You could have told me. At any time, you could have told me," I say, staring back at a man I know is a good man, even if his decisions hurt the hell out of me.

"I tried my damnedest not to make any more mistakes, and I ended up making more of them because of it."

Love stories don't have to be perfect. As long as there's love there. And we had love. We had true love and I know that.

I believe him. Robert means this with every bit of his heart. I can hear it in his voice.

"I just need you to know, I never stopped loving you and I'm sorry."

"And I love you. I know I'll never stop loving you." I swallow down the anguish and add, "We just can't be together."

I wanted this, and I chose this, and it's still painful.

Growing up always hurts, doesn't it? Nothing quite takes the edge off.

Robert gives me a sad smile I know all too well. He's wiped my tears away a lot over the years. He's been there for me. Loving Brody the way I do doesn't make this part any easier.

"That's all right, isn't it?" Robert asks. "That I love you, but I'm willing to step back and know we're not meant to be together like that … but we can—" He pauses, his throat tight and his gaze moving past me to the park. I wish I had something I could tell him, something I could give him to make all this better.

"I want you to know I'll always be here. No matter what happens, Mags. I'll still be here."

"Don't wait for me. You deserve so much more than that." A shuddering sadness cascades through my body. "Promise me you won't. I would never forgive myself."

"I'll be here as your friend, Mags." His smile is tight, but hopeful. "If you could still be friends with me?"

My inhale is shaky, but I nod as fast as I can. My instinct is to hug him, to wrap my arms around his shoulders and bury my head in his chest, but instead I hold my hands together in front of me. "Yeah, friends."

Robert's expression softens with understanding. "You love him, don't you? Like really love him."

I nod, trying to blink away the flood of tears and not making it. "I love him so much I'm scared."

My first love opens his arms wide. It's a sweet, simple gesture, and I take it like a lifeline, holding him like I wanted to just a moment ago. I wrap my arms around Robert's waist and my body melts into the familiar touch. I needed this. Dear God, I needed this.

"I think he's an all right guy, Mags," he murmurs into my hair. With my eyes closed tight, I let him go. I want to tell him I think Brody's perfect for me, but I don't say a word.

"Promise we'll stay friends?"

I can't give up the love I have with Brody, but in the same way, I can't give up Robert's place in my life, either. He's family to me. He's been family even when things got complicated and hard. That makes him Bridget's family too. I'm not about to start taking people away from her, or from me. It would hurt too much, and be for nothing. We're not college kids anymore. We can handle this, because it's what we both need.

"Always," I tell him. And I mean that too.

CHAPTER
Nineteen

Brody

A S A KID, YOU JUST DON'T KNOW HOW MUCH the simple things in life are going to matter. Makes them seem a lot less simple. Nothing's very complicated about Bridget at the playground. I'm guessing most kids want to swing on the swings and climb up the steps. But damn is there something different about seeing it as her dad. She grins at me constantly, the breeze ruffling her hair. I push away every thought of regret from not getting Magnolia's number on that night four years ago, and drink it in.

These are the small moments I've been missing, but I'm not going to miss them anymore.

Tiny little fists grip the chains on the swing and

Bridget asks me to push her. I keep things gentle and calm. I remember flying up practically into the sky, but hell if I'll take that chance. It's a weird contradiction. Bridget seems so big sometimes and I worry I've missed too much of her life. As her hair flies out behind her and she moves away from me, she seems so small.

I wonder if it's always going to be this way. Probably. I shake my head, pushing away the thoughts of her growing up and asking questions about what happened during the first part of her life and why I wasn't there for her. That's not for a long time, but the knowledge still picks away at me.

A flash of sunlight catches my eye. My heart skips a beat at the sight of her. Magnolia smiles from behind her phone, her posture more relaxed than it was before. "I had to capture the moment," she says. "First time pushing your baby girl on the swing."

So she feels it too, how special everything is. Bridget kicks back toward me and I push her again. I joke with her, trying to lighten the moment, "It's not the first time. We started out on the swings. This is at least the second or third time."

Magnolia laughs and that sound brings me more relief than I thought it would.

"You all right?" I ask her, knowing she was just talking to Robert.

She nods and tells me she is, and although

sadness still hides behind her cadence, it's not so heart wrenching.

The breeze toys with the hem of Magnolia's blue dress as she comes close. I offer her one hand, the other still giving Bridget a gentle push. Twining her fingers with mine she tells me, "Tonight I want to tell you my secrets."

"Secrets?" I question, not knowing what they are, but ready to hear it all. "You going to scare me away?" I ask her, keeping humor in my tone.

Her eyes widen with the same humor, but there's always a little truth behind every joke. "I hope not," she says and I feel that truth there. Every small step between us feels like a giant leap.

"Good, 'cause I don't want to go anywhere," I admit to her and she gives me a soft smile. "I do have some bad news, though … I told my mom and she needs a moment."

A numbness flows down my shoulders at the look of fear that swirls in Magnolia's blue eyes. "So she's not going to be coming to the park, but she said she'll still come by later today. She just needs to get a grip on the situation."

"Is she okay?"

"It's just a lot to take in." If I know my mom, she's working her way through her emotions where no one can see her. She'll be here. She'll love Bridget. But right now I bet she's mourning the last three years of not knowing she had a granddaughter. I wish I could change that, but it's in the past.

"Right, understandable," Magnolia responds, but her voice is tight and her gaze is now nowhere on me.

"I figured it would be better to give her a heads-up rather than springing it on her?"

"Of course," she answers but again, the easiness is gone. If she's feeling a fraction of what I'm feeling …

"I think we should head home," she says, holding her arms out to Bridget. "Might be nice to lay down for a nap, Bridgey, don't you think?"

I'll never get over the hint of a Southern drawl in her voice. It makes me feel warm and peaceful. And other things that are definitely not appropriate for a trip to the playground.

"No," shouts Bridget, but she climbs down from the swing. Magnolia picks her up and the three of us head back to where we parked by the restaurant.

There's an odd tension and I don't want a damn thing to do with it, so I wrap my arm around Magnolia's waist and plant a kiss on the crook of her neck. She lights up in an instant, a sweet simper matching the heat in her gaze. I want so badly to say the words I know would make all of this right. Three words I feel in the depths of who I am. She's the first to speak, though, and the moment is lost.

"Thank you for lunch," she says. Like it was a first date or something. *Fuck*. I swallow down my pride and smile back at her. How is it that she still makes me so damn nervous?

"I'd like to come by in a while," I say, rushing out the words after she's got Bridget all buckled in her seat. "Once you're home and settled in."

She lets out a breath with a smile. "I feel plenty settled in with you right now," she admits.

I slip my arms around her shoulders and wrap her in a tight embrace. The words are right there, but they don't come. I know it's because I'm afraid the moment I say them, everything will slip away. There's so much happening so quickly. I can't ruin this. I can't lose her with so much on the line.

Magnolia is only out of sight for a minute before the ache begins. I want to be next to her so much it hurts. My only saving grace that keeps me from second-guessing everything that happened today is that she texts me when she gets home and tells me to swing by whenever I want.

My text back is instant: *Give me an hour*. I just have to do one thing first.

Magnolia pulls open the door as soon as my feet hit the porch, like she was waiting for me, and I'm struck all over again by how gorgeous she is. The blue dress has been replaced with a pair of soft leggings and a cream-colored tunic. Her blond hair falls in loose waves around her shoulders. It's Magnolia's smile that brings it home. All the nerves melt away.

As long as she keeps smiling, it'll be all right.

"Hi," she greets me, those gorgeous eyes traveling down to the bouquet in my hand. It's a riot of pink. Light pinks, dark pinks, with a splash of yellow tulips. I told the lady I wanted something that felt brand new. It seems she read my mind. "Those are so beautiful."

I hand them over and Magnolia buries her face in them to inhale the scent. "And this is for Bridget. I take it she's napping?" There's a lack of a little face peeking around Magnolia's legs and I don't hear the constant chatter of a sweet little toddler.

My toddler. *My* daughter. Well … ours.

"Yeah, she's been down for almost an hour." Magnolia reaches for the gift bag, but I pull it back. "You're not gonna let me see?" Her wide eyes and smile paired with her outraged tone are comical.

"It's a surprise," I tell her and she laughs, rolling her eyes and leading me into the house. Inside, I place the bag on the coffee table and note that it seems so calm and inviting. This is another tiny moment that somehow carries a lot of weight. Gratefulness creates pressure in my chest, and a sense of warmth too. "It's funny how life can change so quick." Voicing it out loud makes it seem even truer. "I want you to know I'm excited, though." I swallow my nerves the second I get out the confession.

Magnolia's gaze meets mine over the bouquet as she stands in the kitchen, pausing for a second before opening a cabinet. "Maybe I don't know what I'm doing, but I swear I'm ready for this." My heart gallops as I watch her pull out a large vase.

"If it makes you feel any better," I admit to her as she turns on the water to fill the vase, "I'm pretty sure I'm going to make a lot of mistakes."

She cracks a smile. "We can make mistakes together then."

As I make my way into the kitchen, the tension builds between us. I wait for her to set down the flowers, and then I do what I've wanted to do since lunch. I run my fingers through Magnolia's hair. She tips her face up to meet mine with no hesitation. Kissing her is the most familiar and new thing I've ever done. Her lips part for me and a soft moan catches in the back of her throat.

"It's easy with you," I murmur against her mouth, letting my thumb that had been resting on her chin trail down her throat. "It feels right. Does it feel right with me?"

Magnolia nods, her breath hitching.

I'm hard as a rock instantly, and I want nothing more than to take her right here and fuck all the worry out of both of us. My eyes close and I groan, hating that I can't do just that.

I wish I didn't have to tell her what I say next, "My mom's coming by."

Her warm laugh is the sound I've waited all my life to hear. "Right now?"

"Any minute. You nervous?" I ask her and she shakes her head. "Well, my mom—"

Magnolia cuts me off with a slow, soft kiss. "I love you," she says after she pulls back. Shock lights her eyes and she's quick to turn away, tucking a loose lock of her hair behind her ear. "And I'm excited to meet your mama."

She's tense and the heat between us intensifies. A smirk slowly grows on my face even though my heart's racing like it's trying to run away from me. She said she loves me. Her cheeks get redder with each passing second as I stand there and stare at her.

"I'm excited for you to meet her too," I say to put her out of her misery and she barely peeks up at me, placing the stems in the vase.

Taking a few steps forward, I close the distance between us, wrapping my arms around her waist and bring her back to my chest. With my lips at the shell of her ear, I whisper, "And I love you too."

Her lips find mine in an instant as she turns in my embrace to face me. With her moan, our kiss deepens and everything is perfect. Until it isn't.

A knock at the front door breaks up our kiss, and I find myself cursing and biting down on my lip as Magnolia wriggles out from under me to head for the door. She opens it with a wide, welcoming smile on her face. My mom's already got a matching one on hers. "Hi," my mom cries, pulling Magnolia in for a big hug. "Hi. You must be Magnolia. Is it time to meet my grandbaby?"

Nerves prick their way down my neck. "How about you walk in and take your coat off first, Mom?" She's a bit much, her own nerves shot too. I don't think there was a way to avoid that, though.

"Sorry, right," my mother comments and walks in, complimenting Magnolia's place.

I told her I loved her. I told her I had no idea about Bridget. But I told her I loved her too. I'm sure Magnolia can tell my mother's been crying. Her eyes are red still.

I want to tell her they're happy tears, but I imagine it was a mix of emotions. It's not every day you find out you had a grandbaby and that you missed the first few years of her life.

"Do you want to," Magnolia says, then gestures to the sofa and we all take a seat. With a tight smile, Magnolia tells my mother, "She's just napping."

"Does she know?" my mom asks and looks between the two of us. "That I'm her grandmom and Brody is her father?" I'm caught off guard by the bluntness of her question, but Magnolia doesn't miss a beat.

"We can tell her when she wakes up," Magnolia says and then looks over her shoulder to me. "If you want?"

Again my heart races and I nod. "Yeah, let's tell her."

"She doesn't sleep for long," Magnolia comments. "I'm sure she'll be out soon."

I start to think it's going to be awkward and regret the decision to tell my mother, but then Magnolia tells her, "You don't know how much I wished I'd gotten your son's number four years ago."

Her voice is tight with emotion and she does that thing where her fingers twine at the ends of her hair. I'm quick to reach out to her, taking her hand in mine.

My mother leans back to look Magnolia over. Pride fills her eyes, and a kind of awe. I know that feeling. It's how I feel when I look at Magnolia. "You raised her on your own?"

"Oh, no." Magnolia shakes her head. She won't deny her history. Everything that has to do with Bridget is special and irrefutable. Even I can see that. "I had help."

Mom glances at me. "It's not the same as having a partner," she says.

Magnolia's eyes glisten. "No," she whispers. "It's not."

"Oh, come here." My mom brings her in for another

big, long hug. "You did a fantastic job, honey. I'm so honored to meet you."

My mother's a lot to handle, but it turns out Magnolia is damn good at handling it all.

Bridget and my mom hit it off. Each of them were happy to have each other. I'm not sure how much Bridget really understands, but she's happy. That's what matters.

Time flies by far too quickly and all too soon, it's both Bridget's bedtime and my mother has to leave for the airport. She contemplated staying longer, but thank God she decides not to cancel her flight. I love my mom, but I want a little time alone to adjust to all of this.

"I'm sorry it went by so fast," Magnolia says as the taxi pulls up.

"We've got time," my mom tells her. "We've got plenty of time. Don't you worry. We've got time."

It feels so damn good to hear her say that.

It's me and Magnolia on the porch, watching her ride drive away. Both her hands wrap around mine and her soft body leans into me when the lights from the taxi fade into the distance.

"I loved today," she whispers and lets out a soft sigh.

I lean down to kiss her at the same time she tilts her

head up to kiss me. The second the front door closes, my patience runs out.

I knead my hands on Magnolia's body and capture her lips with mine. She gasps a little as I push her back against the door and skim one hand up the side of her neck. "Brody," she whispers, not hiding either the lust or the shock.

"Damn. Say that again."

"Brody."

I've never hurried so fast in my life as I do on the way back to her bedroom. Magnolia kicks the door shut softly and strips her shirt over her head, wriggling out of her leggings while I undo my pants. Her eyes stay on me the whole time.

My pants hit the floor, and she's on me. Pushing me back onto her bed, she climbs over me and buries her face into my neck, leaving a trail of kisses.

"Fuck," I groan, loving how she takes control. It feels like heaven to have her luscious body pressed against me. As she moves against me, her pebbled nipples tease my chest. I thread my hand through her hair and pull her face in close to nip her lower lip. I'm never going to stop kissing her. Not until the last breath leaves my body.

Placing a hand between her legs, I feel how ready she is for me. The whimper that slips from her lips is addictive. She needs this as much as I do. Magnolia makes a soft sound in the back of her throat when I push two fingers inside her.

She grinds herself on my palm, eager and needy. It's a gorgeous sight. Her lips are parted from her heavy breathing, her eyes half-shut and her chest flushed.

I'd stay here all day. I'd stay here forever, if that was on the table.

But it's not. We're short on time for the sweetest possible reason. I line myself up with her hot entrance and slowly guide her hips down on my length. Magnolia's muscles flutter around me as her eyes close. Her breathing pauses and I wait a moment, letting her adjust. With both hands on my shoulders, her nails dig into my skin. I lean up to kiss her, deep and full of the longing I have for her.

Slowly she picks up the pace, and with each downward movement, it takes everything in me not to thrust upward.

She's the sight of perfection, riding me like this. Her hands move against my chest as tempting, low sounds escape her. As she gets closer to her climax, her pussy tightening around me, I'm all too glad to take over. I'd do anything for her. In one swift move, I turn us both over, forcing her onto her back and take her mouth with mine.

Every muscle in my body works for her. I want Magnolia to know how much I love her and how much

I need her and how much she's mine. I show her that with every thrust of my hips, making sure to build her pleasure as she tightens around me. Magnolia is going to wring the orgasm right out of me, but first—

Angling my hips a slightly different way, I make more contact with her clit. Magnolia's eyes fly open as she comes. Her hand shoots up to cover her mouth and muffle the sounds. I need a hotel room. I need to take her away when the time is right and get her somewhere she can be loud. As it stands, I drink in every noise she makes.

"I love you," I whisper into her ear, and she clenches around me again, finding her release. Still flushed, still clinging to me, she stares into my eyes and tells me she loves me too.

I hope it stays like this forever.

Epilogue

Magnolia

One year later

THERE'S NOTHING LIKE AUTUMN IN SOUTH Carolina. Trust me on that one. At college, the fall was cold and bright and intense, but it has a gentler feel here by the sea. We've got the same crisp reds and oranges in the leaves, but the nights aren't so frigid. Nothing seems bitter this fall. Some things might be bittersweet, but isn't that how life goes?

Subconsciously, I spin the diamond on my ring finger and Renee laughs. "You look gorgeous, babe. Stop being so nervous."

"It's my wedding day, and it kind of snuck up on me."

"How did it possibly sneak up on you?" Renee faces me in the lobby of the courthouse downtown, an elegant building with white pillars and old Southern charm. Hundreds of people have been married here over the years. Hundreds of brides have probably stood right on this creaky hardwood floor. I hope all of them had a best friend like Renee.

Even if she's lying to me when she tells me she and Griffin are fine. I know there's something going on there.

"Well, once you're pregnant time does funny things, like speed up and go by in a whirlwind."

Little hands on my belly emphasize the point. "Are you gonna have the baby today, Mama?" Bridget asks, her eyes big and round, staring at my belly. Kids don't let you get away with anything. It would have made the waiting easier if we hadn't told her. Oh well. Secrets are hard to keep when they're such happy ones. My six-month bump rounds out the front of my white lace flowing dress. The dress is my *something new* for the wedding. The *something old* is my mother's wristwatch. The *blue and borrowed* is the handkerchief Adeline, Brody's mother, gave me the last time she was here. She said I was going to need it sooner rather than later, and she was right.

"Mama," Bridget repeats her question, bringing me back to the now. "Is the baby coming today?

"Not today," I tell her, ruffling her curly hair. Her

dress is mine in miniature, complete with the delicate straps. She twirls with a laugh.

We kept meaning to plan a wedding, Brody and I, but that's the thing about being so in love. It makes time do funny things. Brody and I jumped into life together without hesitation, like the way we do cannonballs off the side of a sailboat. His brewery has taken off, becoming a favorite destination around town in the evenings. Including the fried pickles. He said we had to have them since it was our first meal together. With my salt tooth, they're my favorite thing on the menu. I never knew how many sporting events there were in the world until Iron Brewery became the popular hangout.

And then we found out I was pregnant. We weren't trying, but we also weren't not trying.

I'll never forget the moment I told Brody the news. I hadn't even had time to come out of the bathroom. He barged in, not knowing I was in there, and found me standing at the sink with the stick balanced on the ledge. "Magnolia," he said, and I met his eyes in the mirror. I didn't have to speak the words, and he knew.

The smile, charming and contagious, grew on his face as he stared down at the plastic stick with its positive indicator. He turned me in his arms and knelt down on the floor, his smile pressed against my belly. I've known a lot of love in my life, but it suffused me in that moment. I had no belly to speak of. I was a month pregnant at most. Brody placed trembling hands over my flat belly and leaned his forehead there too. "I'm going to be here every second," he whispered, emotion thickening his voice. "I'm not going to miss a thing." Hearing him say it healed the last regret in my heart. He couldn't be there for my first pregnancy, but this one—

Well, he's been there for everything. Every baby appointment and late-night craving.

So the plans for a huge wedding didn't come together, but I can't wait for another day to marry him. Good thing I won't have to. We've got a reception planned for next summer and a lifetime together after that.

I take a last glance at my reflection in the window. Bridgey keeps calling us princesses. It's perfection. All of this. The courthouse wedding and Renee at my side, and—

Brody. He steals my gaze from the white of my dress and my heart catches. This feeling is the one I'll never get over no matter how long we're together. He's stunning. Blue eyes and broad shoulders, and a body that speaks of hard work. The new dark suit he's wearing skims strong thighs. Looking at his tight waist, heat curls in my core. That's my soon-to-be husband.

He walks shoulder to shoulder with Griffin, who says something with a smile and Brody laughs. Robert walks in tow with them. A soft ache will always be there for him in my heart. I know he's here for Bridget as much as he is me.

He was the first man in her life and he stands by that. "Whether we're together or not now isn't what matters, Mags," he told me once. "Relationships are. You're my best friend. And I'm not going to walk away just because I can't have you in the same way anymore."

I had no idea how close he and Brody would get. Robert is still one of my best friends and according to Brody, Robert's given him insight into what makes me upset and little things that make me forgive more easily when I'm mad. I rolled my eyes hard at that one. I love how close they are, though. I get Wine Down Wednesdays and Brody goes out with the boys on Monday nights. The "boys" includes Robert. Their genuine friendship makes everything easy.

The rumor around town is that we're a throuple. People talk, and I let them because I'm too busy laughing. I don't care what people have to say. I only care that I have the people I love in my life. All of them.

When the three men push open the front doors, Brody doesn't slow his gait. He strides straight to me and pulls me in for a long, deep kiss. I let out a startled gasp followed by a laugh, but I don't miss a beat wrapping my arms around his strong shoulders.

"Hey," Renee scolds, batting him away with shooing

motions. "You're not supposed to see the bride until she walks down the aisle."

"Too late," Brody says, a gruff edge in his voice. He still smiles at me like he did that first night years ago. The only thing that's changed is that he never takes his hands off of me in public ... or in private. He told me, "I'll never get enough of you," when I tried to shoo him out of bed this morning. There were things he had to take care of at the bar before the ceremony, but the man didn't want to leave. He climbed over me instead so he could kiss down the side of my neck. Pulling at the neckline of my maternity top, he kissed me on the collarbone, and then lower.

Feeling the flush climb up my cheeks, I halt those thoughts where they are and focus on my any-minute-now husband.

"You're the prettiest thing I've ever seen," he murmurs, blue eyes looking deep into mine. "Daddy," Bridget says and pouts. I'm surprised she heard since his voice was so low.

"Except for you." Brody kneels down and scoops up Bridget in his arms while she laughs and laughs. "You're the most beautiful," he tells her sincerely.

"You look amazing, Mags." Robert steps in, slipping his hands into his pockets. His smile is genuine. "I'm happy for you two."

"Thanks." Tears prick my eyes and I wish they wouldn't.

"You really do make a good-looking couple," Renee comments and I don't miss Griffin's focus on her at the word *couple*.

"You need anything before we go in?" Robert asks.

"A picture," I answer suddenly.

"Excuse me." The woman behind the check-in desk looks up, her eyebrows raising in surprise. "Could you take a photo of us? It's my wedding day."

"It sure is, honey." She comes to take my phone with a broad smile and steps back. Robert instinctively moves away, but I grab his elbow and pull him in right next to Griffin, who stands beside Renee.

"I mean all of us," I say. "I want everybody who's important to be in this picture. And you're all important." With an easy exhale, I pat under my eyes, forcing all those emotions down.

"Not now," warns Renee. "Keep your makeup pretty."

"I know. I know," I respond like a petulant child.

The five of us crowd together, with little Bridget right in the middle, and it really does feel like the perfect moment. These are my people. Robert and Renee, my best friends, who would do anything for me and my daughter. Brody, the love of my life. And Bridget, my bright star.

"Did I miss it?" a woman shouts, and I feel Brody perk up at my side, twisting to see who it is.

It's his mom, who got in last night. It's a bit of a surprise and I can't hold back the grin. Behind her are Sharon, Autumn, and Bri, her sister. Brianna's gotten close to us recently, with plenty of drama to spill at Wine Down Wednesdays.

"Mom," he calls, and his face lights up with joy. I bet he doesn't even realize how handsome he is when he smiles like that, or how it makes my heart go pitter-patter. "We said we were going to hold a reception later on for everybody to—"

"Oh, please." She breezes past all of us and pulls Brody down to kiss both his cheeks. "You think I was going to let my only son get married without me there to see it? Hi, sweetheart." She kisses the top of Bridget's head. The two of them are thick as thieves whenever Brody's mom visits. They took to each other right away. Kids can recognize kindred spirits, I think. "Besides, someone has to take pictures." She balances a camera in her hands, winking at me.

A man sticks his head out the door of the courtroom. "Brody and Magnolia?"

In varied sundresses both Autumn and Sharon call out, "Just a sec," as they pick up their pace to get to us.

"That's us," I say, maybe a little too loud. Robert laughs.

"Everybody ready?" asks Renee. "You ready, baby?" She and Adeline, Brody's mom, have each taken one of Bridget's hands, and the three of them look fit to burst with excitement.

"You ready?" Brody whispers, grinning at me while he takes my hand.

"I'm ready," I proclaim, my fingers twining around his.

We lead our group, hand in hand and I didn't expect it to feel like this. It's a shotgun wedding, but the tears come regardless. He's a steady presence next to me as my legs turn weak.

"I love you," he murmurs to me as we go to begin our new lives together.

"I love you too."

Asher

The courthouse is only a block away from where I stand, waiting on my order from the coffee shop. My gaze is focused on one particular woman wearing a beautiful sundress. I know she saw me; she's only looked back once. She looked back, though, and that means something.

I never much liked weddings. My own parents never got married, so I grew up not knowing the point. As I watch the group of women follow Mags and Brody into the courthouse, I have to admit, I get it now. In a way.

The gray clouds are threatening to bring a downpour, but Robert told me Mags said it's good luck if it does rain on their wedding day. If that's true, I need to start standing out in storms. I'm going to need all the luck I can get.

"You going to the courthouse too?" Gail asks me, handing over a tall coffee. I give her a broad smile and shake my head. "I've got work, but I'll be celebrating with them after."

Her red lipstick and pinned-up hair have been Gail's preference since I can remember. Everything about this town has been the same all my life.

Except her. Bri Holloway.

"You think the other couple are going to get married next?" Gail asks me and it's only then that I realize she's still standing with me next to the large paned-glass window. The wedding is the talk of the town after all, so I shouldn't be surprised. According to … well everyone, it's long overdue.

"You talking about Renee and Griffin?" I clarify, giving the nosy woman a side-eye.

She smirks at me and says, "You know I am."

"Well, I don't know much about that," I lie. I know damn well what's going on with them.

"Order up!" someone calls out from the back, and Gail hollers back that she's coming.

"You have a good day, Asher," she tells me, tapping the table before slipping her pen back into her apron.

"You too," I answer her, but my tone slips, betraying me. *A good day* ... If she would just talk to me, if she would just let me explain, maybe then anything would feel good again.

From *USA Today* and *Wall Street Journal* best-selling romance author, Willow Winters, comes a second-chance story with a possessive, filthy-mouthed hero who's not willing to lose the love of his life again.

I've got a thing for men who work with their hands. I thought I learned my lesson years ago. But here I am, back in the small town I grew up in, staring down the man who broke my heart years ago.
I intended to tell him off.
My plan was to flip him the bird and prove to both of us that he hadn't ruined me.
I sure as hell wasn't going to sleep with him.

Until he tells me he's sorry.
Until he gives me that smoldering look I still dream about.
Until he whispers just beneath the shell of my ear … His breath trails down my neck and he leaves an openmouthed kiss right there, in that sensitive spot.
"You have no idea how much I've missed you."

My treacherous heart wants more. More of him. More of us. But there's a reason it didn't work out before and when you don't learn from your past mistakes, you're bound to repeat them.

Don't miss this sweet and sexy romance … Preorder today!

ABOUT THE
Author

Thank you so much for reading my romances. I'm just a stay at home mom and avid reader turned author and I couldn't be happier.

I hope you love my books as much as I do!

More by Willow Winters
www.WillowWintersWrites.com/books